ORDER OF KINGS

THE RISE OF THE PENGUINS SAGA

STEVEN HAMMOND

Rockhopper Books

This is a work of fiction. Any references to historical events or real locales are used fictitiously. Any other resemblances to actual events, locales, or persons, living or dead, are purely coincidental.

Edited by LS King & Murphy Rae with Indie Solutions
www.murphyrae.net
Cover art by Caner Inciucu
Interior layout by Tanya Adams
Exclusive content at:
riseofthepenguins.net

Dedicated to

Those who know a dream is really an idea.

ACKNOWLEDGMENTS

A special thanks to Joshua Muster, for all of his work on my website, press releases, bookmarks, and taking the time to share my events; and all of the loyal Penguinauts. You may be few in number, but your enthusiasm keeps me going. And a special thank you to Lauretta Hobson, a voice from across the pond who reminded me there is no such thing as a void, and who is well aware that penguins don't eat underwater goats with snorkels and flippers. My wife, Joy, who always believes, even when I don't.

And of course Buster Dog, who knows when it's time for a break better than I do.

THE RISE OF THE PENGUINS SAGA

DRAMATIS PENGUINIS

King Penguins of South Georgia Island, Colony of Elinthaw
(Aptenodytes patagonicus)

King Elinthaw—His Majesty of the Order of Kings
Queen Gelika
Admiral Gregor
Vicar Kaff
Captain Thane—Order of Kings
Lieutenant Hally
Lord Keese—Order of Kings
Lordess Tolk—Order of Kings
Elatha-Cadail

The night brings a special misery to the weak.
—Cuasan, Lord of the Underworld

ORDER OF KINGS

CHAPTER 1

Admiral Gregor fought against the fierce wind blowing through a pass in the Allardyce Range of South Georgia Island. Swirling snow and ice, carried down from the highest peaks, obscured his vision. Gregor tightened his eyes against the driving wind, trying to gauge his position. He was close to his destination, but how close he didn't know. He had made this journey a hundred times or more, but during whiteouts, even the most familiar of landmarks appeared foreign. He continued on, trudging his way until his face met a protruding, pointed, wind-worn rock known as Cuasan's Beak. A few more steps, and he would've fallen into a deep ravine and met the rock's namesake, the Prince of the Underworld, on his journey to the Great Sea. Gregor grumbled and took a few steps back. He had his bearings now.

He followed a well-worn path along the mountainsides, complaining about King Elinthaw and his propensity to call these meetings when conditions were at their worst. But Gregor, like all King Penguins, had pride, and no amount of adversity, whether it be from nature, man, or another penguin, could deter a King who had set his mind to a task. Perhaps that was why Elinthaw chose days like this to weed out those who lacked fortitude. Blinding snowstorms be damned, he got to the task of finding his way back.

Gregor trundled back the way he'd come and found his missed turn in no time. He clambered up loose stones, gravel trickling under the weight of his three-feet-tall frame, brusquely protesting each time he slid back. Digging his beak into the earth, he grunted and pulled until at last he surmounted the precipice. How the old and somewhat addled King Elinthaw managed to make the climb was beyond him. He would've guessed the fat senior penguin would have tumbled to his death traversing this path. He berated himself for thinking such profane thoughts; Elinthaw was his king and his guidance had seen to the survival of many King Penguins during the Overlord's ill-advised war. At the very least, he owed Elinthaw respect.

The loose ground gave way to a well-worn stone path, travelled upon by generations of members of the Order of Kings. The wind eased, as it always seemed to do on the summit of Mount Kraysol. Dark forms of angular rock, stretching toward the hazy peach sky, appeared from behind remnants of a shroud of wind-driven snow. Gregor approached the formation, craning his neck to see the top of the odd, jutting stones. He stared at the tips of the natural monoliths and shivered; they always reminded him of the claws of a dying bird, reaching for the clouds a final time before death took it. Maybe that's why the elders had named the sacred meeting place of the Kings the Talon of Wisdom; supposedly, the knowledge of the Ancients and the world became yours the moment before death and the journey to the Great Sea began. *That's a fine time to receive such an education, when it will do you no good,* Gregor thought.

A voice from near the center of the circular arrangement snapped him out of his reverie. "You can stare at it all day and night; the claws won't so much as twitch," a stout, old King Penguin said, his voice carrying forced humor and hope.

"Your Highness," Gregor said, his gaze shifting to meet King Elinthaw's. He stared into the aging king's eyes, a gray haze covering once vibrant yellow-brown irises. Gregor pulled away, looking toward the western sky through the icy dust of the dying windstorm. "I wouldn't have thought a penguin capable of such stealth, especially one who has seen twenty-six winters."

Elinthaw chortled and followed Gregor's gaze to the diminishing sunlight. "I hide in the wind, my old friend. But as sneaky as I may be, I can't hide from the Taker much longer, can I?"

"None can." Gregor kept his eyes on the surrounding mountains. Wisps of snow danced from distant peaks, getting lost among the clouds. "But after twenty-six winters, you've avoided him longer than most."

"He'll catch me before the twenty-seventh, of that I have no doubt. But until that time, we have a meeting to see to."

Admiral Gregor took a step toward the stone columns and spotted Queen Gelika standing by the nearest, watching him. He stopped and turned to Elinthaw, clearing his throat. "Your Majesty, Commander Kiley has chosen to ignore the edict. It appears he has thrown his lot in with the alliance and the Royals." When he looked back, Gelika was gone.

"So he *has* betrayed the Order. We need the Kings under his command. We are weakened otherwise." The old penguin sagged. "This is a dangerous time. Our enemies are multiple; we must defend our nesting grounds."

"From whom, Your Majesty?" Gregor asked, doing his best to show patience. "The Royal Emperors are a defeated clan, whether they know it or not. The humans have their eyes elsewhere. After the battle of South Georgia, I doubt they'll try to return here anytime soon."

Elinthaw grew quiet at hearing Gregor mention the battle. His head lifted with a jerk. "Many died in that wretched battle. I was a fool to ever believe the Overlord. Allies don't fight alone! That's why we make alliances. We aid one another." He looked at the sky, then to the ground, flicking a small stone away with a worn and rounded claw. "I believe Calophus controls the days of a penguin's life. Who other than a trickster would cause the days to crawl when we anticipate fortune, and in a moment of joy, swim past us like the magnificent silver fish?"

Gregor stared at Elinthaw. Mentioning their victory always seemed to push the king into a melancholic rant. "Many were lost, but we came away with a victory, Your Highness."

"They weren't *lost*, Admiral," Elinthaw barked, fury in his eyes. "The dead will not be found at some future point. They were killed, brutally, by those who shared our islands for generations in peace. They were killed by my own stupidity. They were killed by an old penguin who listened to ill counsel. If not for Gelida's sacrifice, many more would have died."

Gelida's sacrifice, thought Gregor. There had been plenty of sacrifice during the two-day skirmish. The admiral felt a familiar rage rise at hearing Gelida being exalted once again. He began to speak but caught himself. Gelida had been the queen's sister, and he was certain that royalty regarded its members higher than a common King Penguin. He shook the last bit of snow from his coat of black and gray feathers. *Let the old penguin mourn however he chooses. Gelida would still be alive if it weren't for him.* "If you'll excuse me, sire. But you *did* call this meeting. Perhaps we should attend."

Elinthaw nodded and walked away without saying a word.

Gregor watched until Elinthaw was greeted by other members of the Order, continuing to stare as the king put on his best show of good humor, an act that had grown tired ten years previous. The admiral exhaled sharply and tried to remember what had caused his growing animosity toward Elinthaw. A subtle click from behind reminded him. "Queen Gelika, shouldn't you be at your mate's side?"

Gelika fixed Gregor with an even stare, letting it linger, thickening the air until she coughed a laugh. "He would hardly notice, Admiral. He's been far too busy mourning my sister's death."

Gregor shot Gelika a questioning look. Was that jealousy he heard? It was no secret the queen had disliked her sister and Elinthaw had taken to protecting the younger sibling from his mate, but was she implying something more? A warning from the past echoed in his head, but he put it aside. "Your sister's death was a blow to us all. She was a natural leader and a strong warrior."

Gelika seemed to bristle at Gregor's assessment but quickly calmed.

She leaned close. "Is that truly what you believe, Admiral? Because I've always felt...." She paused as Gregor shifted uncomfortably. "An attraction to your strength and intelligence. Please don't tell me you're only a brute. How disappointing that would be." She straightened, letting her beak slide against his as she did so.

Gregor rolled his head and cleared his throat. He waited several heartbeats and spoke. "My beliefs are that any words contrary to the throne could be seen as treasonous." He took a small bit of satisfaction when Gelika looked at him sideways, a touch of mischief mixed with doubt between narrowed eyes.

"There are many forms of treason, Admiral... words not the least of them." Gelika's gaze lingered on Gregor for a heartbeat, then she turned to leave.

Admiral Gregor watched her walk away. He let out a long, heavy breath, glad the conversation was over.

CHAPTER 2

King Elinthaw stood in the center of the Talon of Wisdom. The wind tugged at loose pinfeathers, the sheen of youthful feathers lost to age. He plucked a small bit of down from his undercoat and let it loose in the dying gale. His eyes followed the feather to the sky until it disappeared into the coming darkness. He kept his gaze on the sky long after it had gone, becoming fixed on a form riding the wind, gliding on dark wings, far above the assembly, hiding at the edge of sight. A loud call returned his mind to where he was.

"Your Highness, the Order of Kings has assembled," a young King said with an eager and patient voice.

Elinthaw stared, eyes wide, until he'd caught up with what had been said. "Thank you, Lieutenant Hally. I don't know what I'd do if you weren't here to keep my mind on the task."

"It is my duty and my pleasure to serve you, Your Majesty," Hally said, bowing his head slightly.

"If only I had ten of you in my court. But we are each only given one egg." Elinthaw turned his attention to the assembly. "Members of the Sacred Order of Kings, we will forego the usual pomp and get to the business upon us."

"Sire," a shrill, panicked voice cried. "You mean to bypass the invocation as well?"

"Yes I do, Vicar Kaff. Expediency doesn't allow for endless droning to the Ancients."

"Endless droning is better than endless torment in Cayaske for upsetting the Ancients."

"I will make my apologies in the afterlife, Vicar. But I'm sure they will thank me. Your prayers are too long even for those who have eternity." King Elinthaw turned to his lieutenant. "Hally, see that the vicar doesn't interrupt me again."

"Consider it done, Your Majesty." The cheer in Hally's eyes was immediately replaced with restrained violence as he moved toward Kaff.

"My beak is shut, Lieutenant. Not another word. Not another word," Kaff said, retreating into the crowd and ducking behind a column. "I swear to you, not another word."

Satisfied the king's point had been made, Hally returned to Elinthaw's side, his expression calm and cheery again.

Elinthaw looked to the sky, searching for the dark silhouette once again. Satisfied it had gone, he ruffled his feathers and looked to the Order. "I had originally called this assembly to discuss what offensive or defensive options would be available to us once Commander Kiley returned with the forces we deployed to the Penguin Defense Alliance, but I was just informed by Admiral Gregor that Kiley has abandoned the Order and disobeyed the edict."

The news caused a general murmur among the members. After the lieutenant settled the crowd, a self-assured young King came forward, momentarily locking her eyes on Hally. "Sire, may I be allowed a question?"

Hally stepped in before Elinthaw could answer. "Captain Thane, proper decorum insists you address the forum before bringing challenges before the king."

Captain Thane stared down Hally. "I don't need a lecture on decorum, *Lieutenant*. A question is not a challenge. Now let King Elinthaw answer."

Hally narrowed his eyes and puffed his chest. "You are not my commanding officer in this assembly, Thane. I suggest you remember that."

Thane responded with unveiled threat burning in her eyes.

When it looked as if the captain might strike the lieutenant, King Elinthaw cleared his throat. "What is your question, Captain Thane? And see to it that it *is* just a question. I have no time for another debate."

"Thank you, Your Highness," Thane said, letting her gaze linger on Hally for a moment longer before turning to Elinthaw. "Why do we need to discuss offensive options? With the Overlord dead, the Royal Emperors are no longer a threat, and we would do well letting the colony gather its strength and end this needless fighting."

"You're dangerously close to disobeying my order, Captain."

"It was simply a question, Your Highness. Surely you wouldn't put me on the Edge over expressing concern about the wellbeing of the colony." She turned to the other members. Some nodded their approval while others looked away.

"Lieutenant Hally, see that the captain finds her place," Elinthaw said, looking at Thane.

Hally couldn't mask his satisfaction. "It would be my pleasure, Your Highness." He began a slow, deliberate walk toward Thane.

"You'll find I'm not as easily intimidated as the preacher, Hally." Captain Thane carried the look of a penguin wanting to a brawl.

"Need I remind you of the punishment for striking a member of my guard, Captain Thane?" Elinthaw called, his voice wavering under the stress.

Admiral Gregor rushed forward, stepping between Hally and Thane. "That won't be necessary, sire. I can assure you my officers, even those of the Order, would never strike a member of the house of Elinthaw except in self-defense, as our law dictates."

A flash of anger crossed King Elinthaw's face, followed by a look of confusion. He scanned the Order, the ancient assemblage illuminated by a full moon's light reflecting from the snowcapped mountains. He shook bodily, as if ridding himself of a chill, and his confident demeanor returned. "I assume none have objections to the arrest and trial of Commander Kiley?" To everyone's surprise, the subject had changed, and the scuffle between Hally and Thane appeared to be forgotten.

When no objections came, Elinthaw turned to Gregor. "Admiral, I leave it in your charge to seek out your former commander and have him brought in for trial."

"As you have ordered, My King." Gregor offered a high beak salute and turned to Captain Thane. "I trust you can refrain from antagonizing any more of the king's guard?"

"Whatever do you mean, Admiral? I was simply—"

Gregor clicked his beak and gave Thane a wry look, guiding her away from the crowd. "Just restrain yourself, Captain. Elinthaw has been... I don't know, you just saw what happened. It could be his age, or it could something else. Whatever it is, I don't need you to provoke him *or* Hally."

Thane let out a long breath. "You take the fun out of things, Admiral."

"You can entertain yourself by tormenting Vicar Kaff." The assembly erupted into a chorus of calls. "Sounds like the king has called for the vote on his offensive against the Royal Emperors. I'll leave you to your work, Captain."

"The squabbles are the best part," Thane said to Gregor's back.

"Unlike you, I have serious work to do." Gregor walked away, disappearing into the dark behind the stone talons.

Queen Gelika ducked into the shadows behind the admiral.

King Elinthaw watched her go, but paid it little mind. Gelida had been right about her sister; she cared little for anything other than herself. But Gelida hadn't been like that; she'd been loyal and unyielding in her devotion. Had there been any way to do it, he would have made her queen, but it was too late for that. He had allied with the Overlord, and Gelida was dead because of it. A familiar, nauseating pain filled him. It was the Royal Emperors who had caused it all. He'd make them pay. One way or another, they would pay.

King Elinthaw barked at the Order. "No more discussion. We vote."

CHAPTER 3

Gregor got no more than a meter away before he heard Queen Gelika calling him. He spun on his claws to face her. "My Queen, why do you follow me in this forum? Rumors fly through the Order as quickly as a feather caught by the wind."

"Let the rumors fly, Admiral. We have only one life." Gelika stepped closer. "Why waste it worrying what others might think about us?"

Gregor stood, feet planted in the gravelly dirt. His eyes met hers, lingering on the moonlight caught within. "It appears we are going to war. The king has his way with the colony once again."

Gelika pulled back, shaking her head. "I respect your devotion to duty, Admiral, but from time to time, you can afford a break." She looked back at the King Penguins, bickering and puffing their chests in the pale light. "Fools. They'll never learn. Elinthaw has most of them under his sway. You don't get that old without making a few allies."

"You also don't live that long without making at least a beak-full of enemies." He gave the queen an accusing look. "How old is Elinthaw? He was already ancient when I hatched."

Gelika looked at him out of the corner of her eye. "How old did he tell you he is?"

"Twenty-six winters."

Gelika turned her attention to the assembly. "He has outlived most penguins on this island. Only his parents would know for sure. But King Escalefact died when Elinthaw was young, and the queen died after my parents betrothed me to him."

Gregor fought back the urge to offer his opinion on forced pairings. He had learned more about the king in the last minute than he had in his lifetime; he wasn't about to interrupt.

"We are the same age, you and me, Admiral. Almost to the day." She looked toward the dark mountains. "It's strange that fate leads us down the path of most resistance. The things that should be, can't. Some things transcend wanting to become needs, but they're kept just out of reach, so close you can practically nab it in your beak. It's cruel, maliciously cruel, don't you think, Admiral? Decisions you had no part in, dictating the path you follow."

The admiral cleared his throat. "All our paths are directed by the decisions of others, but fate can be made to follow rather than lead." Gregor locked eyes with Gelika, holding her gaze until the call of Thane pulled him away.

Gelika retreated, surveying the darkness surrounding them.

Thane approached, bowing her head in deference to the queen. "Admiral, the assembly has concluded, and you'll be glad to know I did very little to antagonize the lieutenant."

"Very little to you might be a lot to others," Gregor said with no hint of seriousness.

"Always bringing my accomplishments underfoot, Admiral. How can I ever hope to become the Grand Admiral with you making sure I stay down?"

"Other than quashing your dreams, what can I do for you, Captain?"

"Actually, Admiral, I'm here to see the queen."

Gelika eyed the captain for a moment. "Admiral, that is all for this evening."

Gregor bowed his head. "Yes, My Queen." He began to leave but was stopped by Gelika.

"Fate may direct our path, Admiral; however, tonight you should take a king's path. The moon is swollen with light."

Gregor squinted, grumbled, and walked away. He hated cryptic statements.

CHAPTER 4

Admiral Gregor stumbled up the path, intending to discuss Hally's lack of respect toward a fellow officer with Elinthaw. He spotted Elinthaw and Hally in the faint light and began to march toward them to demand a proper recourse. But they seemed to be involved in intense discussion; he hoped maybe his demands wouldn't need to be made after all.

He moved close to one of the stone talons and pressed tightly against it, trying to eavesdrop on the conversation. Despite the wind, Gregor heard Elinthaw praise Hally's treatment of Thane. His temper rose but was replaced with confusion. He'd swear King Elinthaw told Lieutenant Hally he was taking his sojourn and t would return within the week. Why would the king go on leave when he had set the colony on a path to war?

Hally dismissed himself, but Gregor remained at his post. His animosity toward the King rose. The old fool would leave it to his lieutenant to prepare for war. That was unacceptable. He couldn't let this stand. As much as Gregor hated the idea of fighting once again, he and his officer corps were the best hope to keep casualties to a minimum. He swallowed his burgeoning anger. Maybe it was the queen's advances that were making him feel this way about Elinthaw.

Gregor tried to be rid of thoughts of her. He reminded himself once more that no good could come of the path she was trying to lead him down. "The king's path," he whispered, remembering what she had said. He strained his eyes and spotted Elinthaw disappearing over the opposite side of the mountain. It wasn't the way one would take to the shore; it led to the interior of the island, and it was a perilous way at that. Gregor surveyed his surroundings and followed.

He reached the precipice and checking the position of the moon, sat, giving the king time to put distance between them. He fought against his impatience by trying to puzzle out what business any King Penguin would have in the interior, let alone King Elinthaw. A Gentoo he could see doing such a thing; their curiosity was almost as annoying as their verbosity. His gut told him something was amiss. With his patience depleted fully, Gregor continued after Elinthaw.

The wind tugged at Gregor as he stared down an uninviting, steep and narrow path. A few bare spots in the otherwise rocky, gray-brown dirt, speckled with patches of ice, denoted what passed for a trail. He took his first step, brave and bold, without trepidation, and the loose soil gave out under him. He tumbled several feet before coming to rest against an unpleasantly angled boulder. He lay still for several moments, hoping the impact wouldn't dislodge the boulder, causing it to roll down the steep incline and kill the king somewhere far below. When he was certain he hadn't inadvertently set the rock on a course to regicide, the admiral stood and began a more cautious descent.

Moon shadows crept across the partial trail, obscuring any sure purchase for his feet. Icy wind continued to swirl, threatening to pull him off balance and send him plummeting to certain death in the canyon below. He fought against the loose soil and wind while trying to hear whether or not Elinthaw had fallen. Gregor had such difficulty with the downward trek, he was certain the king must've been injured or was lying dead somewhere unseen. Or maybe he'd taken a path Gregor hadn't noticed.

He looked back the way he'd come; moonlight shone on the uppermost part of his journey, illuminating where it had begun over fifty meters above.

No, there was no other way; the narrow pathway hugged the cliff wall at one side and edged a near vertical drop on the other. Either the king was indeed lying dead at the bottom of the canyon, or he wasn't as addled and weak as he'd led others to believe. He put it in his mind to ask Gelika about this later.

Another ten meters and Gregor's claws scraped against ice. He lowered his head to inspect the ice for claw marks and found well-worn grooves from several penguin feet or repeated trips up and down by Elinthaw. He wondered what would motivate the king to make such a hazardous journey more than once. But then again, the ice never thawed in the shadow of the mountain, and the tracks could have been made over a generation, or even longer. A sound beyond the wind pulled his eyes away. He stared at the night sky, motionless, watching clouds roll over the mountains, blanketing the moon's glow. He waited for the noise to repeat, but it buried itself in the gale He placed his foot against the grooves, and followed them down.

Admiral Gregor continued carefully, placing his feet in the tracks of those who had gone before him, peering at the moon as it glanced at him from behind the curtain of clouds time and time again, traversing the night sky until it was hidden by the mountain. He reached flatter terrain, which widened considerably, relieving him of the stress of knowing any misstep could be his last.

There was no ice where he stood, and the air felt thicker with the unmistakable scent of moisture. But the damp air carried a strange smell, like that of decay. Tendrils of fog crept forward, stealing what little light remained. He took a cautious step toward the mist, then stopped. Something inside him screamed an alarm, warning him not to proceed. His conscience told him to continue, find the king and rescue him from whatever trouble he found himself in, but Gregor's instinct won out, and he took a step back.

The sound he'd heard farther up the mountain returned, and this time he recognized it as the sound of beating wings. He strained his eyes to see, but the night only revealed the blue-gray of the misty fog. What sort of bird flew at night? He didn't know the answer; he only knew he had to leave this place. Never in his life had he felt bravado flee from him—not in battle, not in the face of an Orca, and never from the unknown. But he knew he had to go immediately. If the king was in trouble, then let the old fool find his peace in the Great Sea.

He'd turned to begin the long and arduous climb back up when a whisper stopped him.

"*Gregor*," a quiet voice said.

Gregor spun around, narrowing his eyes against the fog. "Your Highness, is that you? Show yourself." The sound of wings overhead drew his eyes up, but nothing could be seen.

"What fear lies within you, Admiral?" the whisper asked, drawn out, almost mocking.

Gregor puffed his chest. "I'm not the one hiding in the night. You should ask yourself who the fearful one is." He waited for a reply but only received silence. "As I thought," he said, turning to leave once again.

A piercing, grating laugh broke the silence, followed by the flapping of wings. "Admiral Gregor, your boldness cannot mask that which dwells within you. I see. I know. Your fear is real."

"You see nothing. Reveal yourself. Or remain a coward in the dark." Gregor stood as strong as he could, but a weakness began to overcome him and with it, the stench of decay grew.

"I'm certain that is not what you want. But... since you asked." A black figure crept forward through the mist, appearing to ripple through the darkness, there and gone, and back again.

"Impossible," Gregor whispered. He made haste up the path but was met by the screaming beak of a Skua. He stepped back, trying to slap it away, and lost his footing, falling to his back.

The large bird pounced on his chest, continuing to screech in his face, carrying on its breath the sickly smell of death of the last penguin chick it had consumed.

He rolled onto his stomach and got to his feet. He ran toward the incline, and the dark penguin, who he'd tried to run from, appeared before him. It stood the same height as Gregor but had a black coat of ragged feathers and eyes as white as any snow he had ever seen. "Cuasan," Gregor said.

The white eyes grew wide. "Cuasan fears me," the dark penguin said with a disturbing laugh, and then it screamed the call of the Skua.

Gregor tried to slap him aside, but his flipper refused to rise. The world around him spun. His stomach lurched, emptying its contents at the dark penguin's feet. The dark penguin's laugh cut through him, a deprived, cackling, insane laugh. Gregor's eyes lost focus, followed by his back hitting the ground. And then the darkness took his sight.

CHAPTER 5

Three members of the Order, including Thane, surrounded Gelika as she tried to make her way down to the shore. She stopped, regarded each of them, and resumed her walk. "Not here. Wait until we get down the mountain."

"We need to speak with you. This is of the utmost urgency," said a penguin whose girth exceeded most penguins the queen had ever seen.

"As I surmised, Lord Keese. We share the same need. However, we must be sure we are not being watched. Captain Thane, trail us until we reach the grotto near the east shore." Captain Thane, the one member of the Order of Kings whom the queen trusted wholeheartedly, owing in no small part to the faith Admiral Gregor had in her, looked over Keese and his colleague, Tolk. Keeping her eye on Tolk a moment longer, she fell into the shadows without a word.

Gelika hurried down the slope with Tolk keeping pace and Keese, breathing loudly, huffing complaints while trying to stay on his feet. "You know, Keese, it wouldn't hurt for you to skip your usual second or third meal from time to time."

"My aggrandizement isn't beyond most others in the colony," Keese panted.

"Your *aggrandizing* makes you breathe like a spouting Orca. And most others in the colony aren't spouting on my neck."

Keese snorted beneath a huff. "Penguins aren't mountaineers, My Queen. We're swimmers; we should have our meetings on the sea rather than having to climb halfway to the stars."

"Tell the king," Gelika said.

"I'm telling the queen. That should be enough," Keese said right before toppling forward. He looked up to find Gelika standing over him with a scoffing look. "I told you we don't belong in the mountains."

"Some more than others." After Lord Keese found his feet, Gelika slowed her pace and glanced at Tolk, who seemed to want to say something. "You don't have to be cautious just because I'm the queen. Speak what's on your mind."

"Of course, My Queen," Tolk said, looking away.

"Well?" Gelika said when Tolk remained silent.

Tolk cleared her throat before speaking. "I mean no discourtesy, but it seems that Lord Keese doesn't speak to you like one should. Back home we were always told if we should ever meet the king or queen, we should regard them—you—nearly as high as the Ancients."

Gelika sighed. "You've made your way into the Order so quickly, I sometimes forget you only came here one winter ago. It's good to know all refugees from the Falklands don't regard us as low as Kiley does. You're correct, Lordess Tolk. In most situations, publicly I should say, royalty should be regarded in such a manner. And as you know, Keese usually does. But I've known him since I was hatched, so he is allowed certain liberties." She gave Keese a wry look.

"I was crèche-minder to the queen when she was nothing more than a ball of brown fluff. Why, the guano that penguin—"

"That is all Tolk needs to know, Lord Keese." Gelika's tone let him know he had pushed the boundaries far enough.

With the exception of Lord Keese's frequent tumbling and exhaustive breathing, they travelled the rest of the way in silence. After a brief swim, they arrived at a cavern masked by sea spray and the night.

Large waves, assisted by the full moon, crashed against remnants of the island's volcanic history, each collision pulling pieces of igneous rock into the surf. Captain Thane rode the waves into the grotto, sliding off breakers and landing feet first with the casualness of one who had mastered the sea and any doubt in her ability.

"I trust you had no problems?" Gelika asked.

"None, My Queen. The mountain has been quiet. With the exception of a lost Skua, one would think nothing lived on this island at night."

"A Skua?" Gelika looked through the mist, trying to see the night sky, but they were well hidden. She doubted anything could see in. She turned to find Thane giving her a curious look. "One can never be too sure, Captain."

Keese interrupted any further discussion of other birds. "My Queen, may we be allowed to speak candidly?"

"That's why we're here, Lord Keese."

"Something must be done. King Elinthaw will see to our end. We are too few after the previous campaign, and the fervor for war has died in most Kings."

"Lordess Tolk, Captain Thane, I take it you two feel the same as Keese?" Gelika led the group higher up the rocks as she spoke, trying to get to a place where the crash of the waves didn't drown their voices. The pair nodded in unison, and the queen nodded along with them. She beckoned them to follow her, leading the group to a recess where the cave walls muffled the sound of the surf.

Only the slightest glint of eyes could be seen in the darkness as Queen Gelika examined the others. Once she said her piece, it would never be undone; she would lead the Kings on an unprecedented course which none would be able to return from. She clicked her beak, her nervousness intensifying her indecision. It was already too late to turn back. "The king's mind has gone weak from age. I agree he will lead us to our end. He must be stopped. He must be stripped of his authority."

A silence hung over them, thick with the anticipation of what would be said next and by whom. Captain Thane was the first to break it. "I'm with you to whatever end we should meet, My Queen."

Lordess Tolk was next. "My colony on the Falkland Islands suffered heavily from our participation in the war. Kiley has taken what few of us remain on a crusade to the North. I didn't come to your home to participate in an uprising. But since I have been accepted into the fold, I cannot stand by while the mistakes of the past are repeated. The Falkland refugees will do what we can to help save our clan."

"Lord Keese, it's not like you to let others speak without interruption," Gelika said, searching for his eyes in the gloom.

"I feel heaviness in my heart over it coming to this, My Queen. But Elinthaw must be made to see the errors of his ways. I will see to it the Guild of Gatherers and Surveyors will be with us."

Gelika nodded, not feeling the need to reaffirm their choices. "Captain Thane, do you think Admiral Gregor will be with us on this endeavor? I have no doubt you could take command of our military if needed, but it will be much simpler with the admiral's endorsement."

Thane moved in, nearly bumping the queen. "You know better than most the admiral's loyalty is to the colony first and king second. You also know he is stalwart in his duty, and disobedience is as foreign to him as flight. But you and I both know of his growing frustration with King Elinthaw. If the majority of the colony is behind us, I'm certain he will follow our lead. But he must be made to see this is what the colony wants. We want new leadership, not old wars."

With the veil of doubt lifted, Gelika felt a new weight pressing on her; the weight of responsibility if it came to violence. "What we are about to embark on has never happened before. There has never been an act of rebellion in the Order of Kings since its founding on Insula in Medio Omnium. My wish is for Elinthaw to see his error and step down. However, I doubt he will be eager to relinquish his authority. Again, if we can avoid any act of violence, it is my wish we do so."

"I doubt most of the members of the Order of Kings will put up a fight when they see what they're facing. However, I beseech you, My Queen, can we make an exception in the case of Lieutenant Hally?"

"I predict Lieutenant Hally will give us more trouble than the king. To that end, you may slap the beak from his face, Captain Thane." Captain Thane's celebratory reply gave Gelika a small laugh, but the seriousness of the situation they found themselves in brought her back to stoicism. "See to it that everything is in place by the fourteenth tide beginning tomorrow. We need to make this as smooth as possible. We will meet again on the seventh ebb. Go, and be cautious."

Before falling into the sea, Queen Gelika asked Captain Thane to wait. "Do you truly believe Admiral Gregor will join us?" the queen asked.

"I think you know the answer as well as I, if not better. When the time comes, I believe he will follow his heart. Sleep well tonight, Gelika. It will likely be our last rest for some time." Captain Thane bowed and jumped into the receding surf.

"I'll sleep, but not before I talk to the vicar. I'll need the blessing of the Ancients," she said to herself, and then followed Thane into the waves.

CHAPTER 6

The cold sea breeze, accompanied by a soft, smooth, warm touch across his beak, caressed Admiral Gregor into the waking world. His mind resisted the call, wanting only to stay in the restful peace of deep slumber. He responded with only the smallest of movements in reply to the invitation to consciousness. It was enough to make him feel the dull ache coursing through him. But still he resisted waking. The warm, moist touch returned, this time accompanied by a guttural rumble, transitioning into a flapping, nearly flatulent popping, terminating in an alto squeal.

Gregor's eyes popped open in alarm. He dug his beak into sandy earth and pushed himself from his stomach to his feet in a blink. His legs trembled with adrenaline. Through the hazy vision of sleep, he spotted an enormous gray, blurry, blob in front of him. The form growled again, and Gregor squeezed his eyes closed to clear the fog. When he opened them, the gray blob was still a blob but had a face. Dark eyes peered at him over a wide, bulbous, whiskered snout which hung down, hiding an even wider mouth with crushing canine teeth.

The admiral shook his head clear, standing strong against the bull Elephant Seal. "Stone, haven't I asked you not to do that? I can wake up on my own."

Stone let out a grumbling, percolate noise, then flopped his head on the beach, assuming his duty of lying on the sand for the day.

Gregor stretched his neck, relieving himself of the final traces of sleep. He looked around, checking the position of the sun. Concerned, he turned to Stone. "When did I get back? Or better yet, how did I get back?"

Stone opened one eye, blew out a puff of air, and closed his eye again.

"You know that's why I gave you your name. You lay on the beach, as still and talkative as a stone."

The large Elephant Seal squinched open an eye, turned his head a different direction, and let out an offensive noise.

"Some help," Gregor said. He shook his feathers and felt the unusual ache in his body. He tried to remember what had happened, but it felt like a distant memory, hiding in the shadows of his mind. No matter how hard he tried, all he *could* remember was being knocked down by a bird or a penguin after following Elinthaw down a mountainside. "It couldn't have been a dream. I wouldn't be sore if it were."

He contemplated what to do. There was only one penguin who could give him the answers he needed. "Stone, I'm going to see Vicar Kaff."

Stone replied by not making the slightest motion.

"It's always a pleasure talking with you, my friend. I never have to worry about an argument."

Gregor searched the pebbly beach and rocky inclines, and across gentle slopes which carried patches of green and purple Alpine Cat's-tail, resting beneath majestic, snow-capped peaks which themselves rested under the firmament of pure blue. His extensive search was rewarded when he spotted Vicar Kaff in the distance, adamantly waving his flippers, as he often did when someone suggested he do something that might require some effort on his part. His tormentor was none other than Queen Gelika. The admiral hesitated. He wasn't sure he had the patience to handle her intentions, but he needed to talk to the vicar to make sense of the previous night. The Ancients knew Stone would be of no help.

He slowed his pace, taking in the scenery leading up to Mount Kraysol, his eyes following the trail to the Talon of Wisdom. He became lost in thought, trying to pry pieces of memories from where they hid in his mind. Gregor took in the sights, watching the wisps of clouds appear and disappear near the summit. "Why couldn't the weather have been like this yesterday?" he said to no one. He tried to turn his attention back to where he was headed, but he couldn't pull away from the clouds. He stared at them, waiting for something. And in his mind, he saw the mist and the form hiding within from the night before. A chill coursed through him, and the memory ended. He strained to get it back, to find out where it led. Someone calling his name broke his focus.

Admiral Gregor shuddered. Vicar Kaff and the queen were walking toward him. He let out a heavy breath and firmed his resolve. "Queen Gelika, what a surprise it is to find you in counsel with the vicar."

"Do you view me so lost and beyond redemption, Admiral, that not even the Ancients would give me guidance?"

"Most of us carry something within ourselves to which redemption is a questionable endeavor at best," Gregor said, matching the queen's less than serious tone.

Vicar Kaff's head bounced between the two, trying to decipher their banter.

Gelika's eyes brightened at Gregor's reply. She looked at Kaff, who appeared on the brink of breakdown. "As it turns out, Admiral Gregor, I was not seeking counsel. I am here advising the vicar on matters of the throne."

Kaff looked at Gregor with wide eyes. His beak parted as if to speak, but it snapped shut with a click.

"Am I privy to these matters, My Queen?" Gregor asked.

"You may be or not. Time will tell. Why have you sought me out? Did you discover anything of interest on your journey home last night?"

Gregor's eyes narrowed and his relaxed stance grew tense. He looked toward the mountain as if waiting for something. He fell back into his memories until again being interrupted by the queen.

"Is there something you learned, Admiral?"

The vicar's expression held traces of fear and doubt. "Actually, My Queen, I, too, am here seeking the counsel of the Ancients."

Gelika glanced at the ground. "Perhaps the vicar can help us both," she said.

"Perhaps," he said in a tired voice.

"I bid you good day, Admiral." She started forward but stopped and leaned into Gregor.

Here it comes again, Gregor thought. He wasn't in the mood for her flirtations, and he thought about telling her so this time, but the advances never came.

"You know, my friend," Gelika said in a whisper, "we may find the same answer to different questions."

It was Gregor's turn to find the ground interesting. He stared at the pebbles and sand until Kaff spoke.

"What do you want of me, Admiral?" Kaff said, his voice carrying an anxiety greater than normal. "I do have things to do too, you know." He began walking toward a nearby outcrop of crumbling, dark rock.

"What lives in the mountain?"

Kaff stopped. He stiffened. After a moment of quiet, he let out a shallow breath. "Many things live on a mountain, Admiral. This is not an answer only the Ancients can give," he said, not turning to face Gregor.

"I didn't ask what lived *on* the mountain, Vicar. I asked what lives *in* the mountain."

Keeping his back to Gregor, Kaff shuffled away. "Nothing lives in a mountain, Admiral. Now if you'll excuse me, I have no more time for riddles."

"Hold it right there. Don't you walk away from me, Kaff."

"I am not subject to your command, Admiral. I answer only to Huhellsus and the Great Giver," he said, picking up his nervous pace.

Gregor rushed forward and stepped in front of Kaff. "Then beseech the Ancients and find me my answer if you don't know." His eyes narrowed, looking down at the smaller penguin. "But I feel you do have my answer."

Kaff put his head down and pushed past Gregor. "I know nothing, Admiral Gregor. You've asked your question, now go back to commanding your underlings. I have nothing to do with this." He hurried off and stumbled over a small rock, giving Gregor the chance to block his path again.

"You're not telling me something, Vicar. Tell me what you know," Gregor demanded, frustrated by Kaff's evasions.

Kaff stared at Gregor for several moments. "No, Admiral. Now really, I must be going."

The vicar tried to get past him, but Gregor prevented it no matter which way he went. "I can do this all day and all night. You can save both of us the time and trouble if you just tell me what you know."

"Admiral, please. I have nothing to tell you," he said, avoiding eye contact.

This time Gregor let him pass. Kaff ambled away, and a memory returned. "I saw a shadow in the mist. White eyes. A Skua."

Vicar Kaff's body went rigid. He slowly turned around. "It was a dream, Admiral Gregor. That's all it could be."

"No. It felt like a dream this morning, but it wasn't. The memories are coming back."

Kaff approached him, looking at him out of the side of his eyes. "Memories? When did this happen?"

"Last night."

Kaff pulled his head back. "It couldn't have. You may have memories from long ago, but last night is impossible."

Gregor thought about it. He remembered talking to Gelika after the assembly. What had she told him? He strained, digging, trying to grab hold of something.

Vicar Kaff stared a moment longer. "I really must go, Admiral. And please don't block my path. It will—"

"Path?" Gregor asked. The memories came flooding back, but as they came, he almost wished they hadn't. "That's it, Vicar! I followed King Elinthaw down the path on the backside of Kraysol. I was attacked, first by a Skua, and then by something much more sinister. A penguin who moved with the mist. It had white eyes. I remember now."

"What you say you saw can't be. He would be impossibly old by now. And even then, it was only legend."

"What was legend? Who?" Gregor asked, almost pleading. "Something happened last night. Something that seemed unreal but was real."

Kaff shook his head. "It's just a legend. A forgotten myth."

Gregor clinched his beak. "Please… I need to know. If there is something up there, and it has done something to the king. We need to do something about it."

Kaff backed away, nodding. He looked toward the summit of Kraysol. "Follow me, Admiral. I must give you something."

Gregor looked to the top of the mountain. It seemed darker, ominous. Clouds rolled over the summit. The cold air cut through his thick layers of fat. Kaff hurried off, and he moved to catch up with him.

CHAPTER 7

Vicar Kaff led Gregor to the back end of a shallow cave. He rummaged through several piles of small stones on the ground, then sifted through a collection of driftwood and plastics that had washed ashore before returning to the stones. "It has to be here." He straightened and scanned the cave.

"What are you looking for? Maybe I can help," Gregor asked, wanting to speed things along.

Kaff looked at him but was lost in thought. "Ah!" he exclaimed and hurried toward a flat board worn smooth by the sea. He nudged the edge with his beak, flipping the board over. "It's in here."

Gregor looked over Kaff's shoulder as he plucked pieces of sea glass from the sand. "What you experienced was a vision of the past."

"A vision of the past?" Gregor repeated doubtfully.

"Yes, yes. A dream from a different time."

"It wasn't a dream, and it happened last night."

"Admiral Gregor, you came to me for answers, and I am giving them to you. The penguin seen in your dream has been dead for a generation. And even then, he was considered a myth."

"If he was a myth, then how could I dream about him?"

"All myths and some legends have their origins in truth, Admiral."

"Whether or not it was once real still doesn't explain how I dreamed something from before I hatched. You're wrong, Vicar. I came to you for help, and instead you give me fables and legends."

Kaff continued to pull pieces of smooth glass from the earth. "Dreams are sometimes the memories of those who came before us. Other times, they're warnings or answers our waking mind can't comprehend. And sometimes they are just dreams. But you dreamt of one who died before you lived. And that one was a certain evil—a-ha! There you are."

Gregor looked expectantly at the object Kaff pulled from the ground.

Vicar Kaff laid a piece of smooth green glass at Gregor's feet. "This is a Bakorpheous crystal. They are left on the shore by The Great Giver. This is a rare color. Most come to us lacking any color, or are the color of the ground. This is a gift, and it denotes peace for a troubled mind. In your case it will protect you from the lost memories of the past until they find their way into the current, to be taken to their former owners in the Great Sea."

Gregor gave the glass a skeptical look. "It looks like something from the world of man."

Kaff shot a look at Gregor. "Your blasphemy will visit you in Cayaske."

He let out a long breath. It was apparent the vicar didn't believe him or was trying to hide something. Gregor leaned toward the latter. With the path to wisdom from the Ancients closed, he changed the subject. "I thank you, Vicar. Perhaps I will rest easy tonight. But before I go, why don't you tell me what the queen wanted with you?"

Kaff flipped the wood back on top of his precious sea glass and looked outside the cave. "I don't intend to be caught up in these matters, but she has gotten the idea of asking King Elinthaw to step down in her head. I advised her to commune with the Ancients over her choice before rushing to action."

Gregor nodded. Now he knew why she was showing interest in him. If the king refused, she would need the backing of the military to force him out. His anger rose. True, he doubted the king's leadership abilities; he was half-blind and half-witted from age, but Gregor hated the idea of being used. And to think he'd nearly allowed himself to fall for it. "I'll speak with her," he said, and spun around to leave.

"Your Bakorpheous, Admiral. Don't forget it; you'll need it," Kaff said.

Gregor took the glass in his beak and stormed out of the cave.

CHAPTER 8

"**A**dmiral," Captain Thane called over a cacophony of over one hundred thousand, squawking King Penguins.

Gregor didn't break stride. If he'd heard her, he didn't acknowledge it. He continued down the shallow slope of a gray hillside. Thane grunted. She would have to catch him if she wanted to talk to him. Judging by his stride and the way he carried himself, looking every bit like a pent-up storm ready to release a deluge of anger, she hesitated. She had seen this side of him before, and even though it was rarer than a blood moon, it was enough to make her second-guess approaching him. But she had no choice.

"Admiral Gregor," she called as insistently as she dared.

Gregor jerked. For the briefest of moments, Thane thought he was going to acknowledge her. He pretended not to hear her instead. "I hate when he's in this mood," she growled quietly, knowing she'd have to chase him down.

Thane pushed through crowds of penguins, trying to be polite but more often than not having to nudge someone aside. Some barked insults at her for her trespasses until they realized who they were besmirching. Some didn't care who she was and continued to spout verbal abuses at her. She promised to remember them the next time they were in need of conscripts.

When she finally broke free of the multitude, Gregor had put much of the beach between them. She hurried after him, calling his name while not caring about the irritation rising in her voice. He disappeared over a low rise, and Thane gave up on any pretense of respect, berating the admiral with a harangue of conspicuous profanity. She overtook the rise to find Admiral Gregor waiting for her. She winced and looked back the way she had come in case she needed an out.

Admiral Gregor set the Bakorpheous stone down. "Did you really liken your commanding officer to an Orca's—what was the word again?"

Thane spied the piece of green glass and cleared her throat. "No need to bring up past transgressions, Admiral. Like the proverb says, a moment ago is a day ago, and it is a moon, a winter, and a lifetime ago. Best we keep it there."

"That proverb was spoken by a Hoiho. They're too forgiving for my taste."

Thane ignored the statement. "Are you going to tell me what has your tail feathers matted? I've chased you halfway to the Falklands, trying to catch you."

"Good day, Captain," Gregor said, picking up the glass.

Thane stepped in front of him. "You know I'll just follow you to your nest. And Stone likes me better than you. He'll pin you down until you tell me what's bothering you or until you run out of breath."

"Stone will do no more than blink and pass air," Gregor said after dropping the Bakorpheous.

"Still, that'll be bad enough. Are you going to cough it up, or do I have to get Stone?"

Gregor lowered his head in defeat. "You're far too persistent for your own good."

"Some would say that's a good quality," Thane said, settling in next to Gregor, still looking at the glass.

"Some would." Gregor followed her eyes. "It's a Bakorpheous stone. Kaff gave it to me. It's supposed to protect you from something or other."

"Kaff? I've never known Kaff to be generous. What's the catch?"

"It's anyone's guess," Gregor said, shrugging. He stared across the beach, following the blanket of squawking penguins to their edge near the slope of Mount Kraysol. "The beach used to be much more crowded. But that was before Elinthaw's bargain with the Overlord."

"We've lost a lot of good Kings." Thane looked at the sky. It was time to see where her friend and commander's loyalty rested. She didn't know what she'd do if they found themselves on opposite shores. "King Elinthaw is about to make the mistake again. Many more of us will die. And to be honest, Admiral, I'm not willing to fight a losing battle, nor am I ready to fight a costly victory. The Royal Emperors are still too strong. And they still have the backing of the alliance…"

"What do you suggest, Captain? That confounded Order of Kings backed Elinthaw with the majority vote. If I don't follow the king's orders, I'll be put to the Edge for treason. And then there's Kiley to deal with. By all accounts, the Kings under his command never received orders to withdraw."

"I doubt they will fight against their own clan."

"As do I. But I have no desire to go to war against the Chinstraps, or Adélie, or even the Gentoo. The only path we have is to wrest control of the Kings from Kiley and have *him* put to the Edge. That is if King Elinthaw doesn't see our colony destroyed first." Gregor stood and stared across the landscape.

Captain Thane followed his lead. "What if I said there are plans in motion to have King Elinthaw removed?"

"By whom?" Admiral Gregor asked, spinning toward Thane.

Thane stepped back. Once she said it, there would be no going back. "Queen Gelika aims to have Elinthaw removed, whether by his stepping down or through force of will. There are Lords of the Order who are behind her on this."

Gregor looked at the ground, shaking his head. "It's as I thought."

"What do you mean?" she asked, unable to mask the pensiveness in her voice.

"Queen Gelika, and her... her advances." He looked away. "I almost thought for a moment...."

Thane stepped closer. "Gelika has no desire to be Elinthaw's queen."

"Nor does she have the desire to be mine," Gregor snapped. "She made it seem.... She only wants the forces I command in case it comes to a coup."

"That's not true and you know it, Gregor. I see the way she looks at you. It's genuine."

"Yes, she genuinely wants the military to back her." Gregor stomped away and then stopped to face Thane. "I was a fool to think of it any other way. But I'm a fool who won't be fooled. She will get no support from me."

Thane watched the Admiral in disbelief. When he stopped ranting, she began hers. "It's true you are a fool. A ridiculous, stubborn, blind fool. What do you think would happen to her if the king found out about her feelings toward you? And of course she needs the military, but she needs you more. I've known you too long; you can't hide what you feel for her from me. If you walk away from this now, if you walk away from her at a time when she needs you to be strong but silent, you'll live the rest of your life next to an old Elephant Seal until you turn to sand."

Gregor stared at Thane, his beak quivering, trying to find the proper retort. "Stone is my friend."

"And he'll be your only one when this colony is led to its death by King Elinthaw. Though I'm sure even he'll see how stupid you've been." Captain Thane grunted in frustration.

Admiral Gregor growled and turned to leave, making a hasty retreat.

"Don't forget your Bakorpheous crystal. Maybe it can protect you from yourself."

Gregor picked up the glass and marched away.

CHAPTER 9

After spending a good portion of the day walking the hillsides, considering his conversation with Thane, Admiral Gregor dropped the green sea glass on his nest and fell in next to Stone. The old bull Elephant Seal, still wet from his afternoon foraging, snorted in response to his arrival.

He stared across the horizon and listened to the cacophony of Kings rising over the surf rolling against the easy beach, making its way to his isolated edge of shore. Stone rumbled a pitiable call, raising his head high and then letting it fall to the ground. Gregor followed Stone's gaze to the empty beach south of them. He gave him a scratch with his beak, and Stone grumbled a mournful appreciation. There were no other Elephant Seals on the beach; they had gone to sea with their pups, but Stone hadn't gone. He was too old to fight for dominance against the much younger and stronger bulls, and as a result, he had been forgotten and left behind.

The admiral had no way to know Stone's age. The bull's body carried innumerable scars from countless battles with other bulls over the course of his life. If each scar he carried accounted for a year of his life, Gregor would assume he was well over one hundred winters old. He knew Stone wasn't, and he didn't care. Stone was his silent friend, and Gregor guessed he was the same for Stone. The two sat or lay on the beach, one or the other making an occasional noise the other couldn't comprehend but meaningful to the issuer, watching the night fall until they could finally hear the waves over the now quiet and sleeping penguins.

The heavy, restful breathing escaping his companion lulled Gregor to the edge of sleep. His mind fell on Gelika, and for a moment, he was angry at the thought of her manipulating him. He remembered what Thane had said. He *was* stubborn. He knew that much about himself. But foolish? He was no fool, or at least not a big enough fool enough to act foolishly. He decided to give thought to reconsidering his stance against the queen. The day's events had proved too great an obstacle for his continued deliberations. His head fell forward, beak against chest, and the night chased away his waking troubles.

^^^

The whisper didn't wake him, but it persisted until Gregor rose. It called his name, cutting through the din of surf and the night wind. The quiet call sounded familiar; more like a memory than a voice from the present. Still sleepy, he couldn't place where he had heard it before. Nevertheless, the voice was comforting, almost paternal. Whoever it was, he had to follow the call.

He stumbled through the depression beside him, left vacant by Stone. It must be later than he'd thought. In addition to his late afternoon feeding run, Stone usually went hunting in the morning just before dawn, while the others slept. Gregor stared at the emptiness until the whisper beckoned once more. He followed it blindly.

The voice continued to call, keeping just out of sight, hiding in the predawn gloom. He wanted to turn back and return to sleep and dreams, but he felt compelled to carry on. Whoever hid on the edge of his vision needed a good reprimand for waking him and rudely not answering his questions. Had he called to this crier? He was sure he had. Why wouldn't he have? You didn't get awakened by a stranger and not ask who it was. He remembered the familiarity and decided he hadn't needed to. Whoever it was, his fatigued mind had simply forgotten. Gregor continued up the hillside without hesitation.

The laborious climb terminated beneath the summit of Mount Kraysol. A hundred meters further up the mountain the stone spires of the Talon of Wisdom stretched to the moon; a hundred meters below was King Elinthaw's throne. Gregor stood in the Court of Sparroth, named for one of the nine Ancients of Judgement. He was alone, waiting for whoever had led him this far to reveal himself. He felt a certain wrongness, and once again doubt washed over him. Had he called out before, and why did it matter? His beak had parted to demand an answer when he heard his name above the wind. The voice felt closer this time.

Gregor twisted on his clawed feet, wary but uncertain why he would feel alarmed. He took a slow step toward the speaker, straining his eyes to see who stood in the darkness. He looked at the moon for aid, hoping it would shine its weak light on whoever owned the whispers. He followed the moon across the sky until it hid behind the mountains. The speed at which it moved didn't concern Gregor. The moon was in the sky, so it must fly like the birds.

He took another step, and the whisper grew louder. Gregor recognized it immediately as his father's voice. He shook his head. It couldn't be; both his parents had died before the war, but for some reason, it made sense. Of course his father would be in the shadows; he had died and gone to the Great Sea. It must be dark there.

"Good. Come to me. Let me see my son, who has become Admiral," his shadow father said.

Gregor snorted a laugh, feeling at ease. From what he remembered, his father was a keen officer and strict in duty. He took another step and cried out in alarm. His father had died *before* the war. There had been no militia in place before Antaean's edicts to the alliance. Why would he think his father had been an officer? "You're not who I think you are? You can't be." His own voice struggling to achieve a whisper.

His father called to him again, this time sounding like Gelika. "I'm sorry, Gregor. You know what would happen if we revealed ourselves."

Gregor nodded. Now it made all the sense in the world. Gelika couldn't risk being seen alone with him during the day; King Elinthaw had too many spies in place. She'd had to disguise herself as his father. He could see her now, just on the edge of sight in a cloud of dusty snow blown by the mountain winds. "Wait," he said, finding his voice again.

Snow-shrouded Gelika turned back. "No. Come with me, and I promise you'll never want to sleep on an empty beach again."

Gregor hurried to catch her. The words "beach" and "empty" swirled through his head. If Gelika had wanted to see him, she would have come to his spot beside Stone. He stopped. His head ached, trying to decipher the truth dancing in the recesses of his mind. She wouldn't risk upsetting the king by bringing Gregor so near the throne.

"Admiral Gregor," King Elinthaw said. "Is this why you abandoned me, so you would take my place at the queen's side?"

"No. No, my worship. I am your faithful servant." Gregor bowed his head. "Any thoughts of the queen are of the purest form."

"Why do I doubt these words?"

The sun rose as rapidly as the moon had set, blinding Gregor and hiding the King in its corona as it flowered over the highest peaks. Gregor seethed at the bright king's accusations. "You dare speak to me of betrayal? You, who had abandoned the queen in favor of her sister. The throne is soiled, the Order of Kings is besmirched, and the integrity of our kind will be cast in doubt because of the actions of a king too proud to face his failures."

The dark silhouette of the king appeared from the bright white of the sun. He strode forward, strong and confident. "Are you challenging my authority as king? It is a king's prerogative to do as he wishes. And I shall use that right to return your challenge. Come, let us trade beaks and decide who would be best to rule."

The admiral squinted against the sun's glare. If it was a fight the old fool wanted, then Gregor would give him one and rid the colony of this madness once and for all. He rushed forward, trying to see through the dazzling rays of light, anticipating Elinthaw's first strike.

From a tired, quiet spot in his mind came a shouted warning. Gregor stopped, looking around in confusion. This wasn't right. The king had taken leave; he couldn't be in this place. His conscious self fought to grasp reality. It latched onto something familiar, both new and old. He remembered the gift given to him by Kaff—the green glass of Bakorpheous crystal. The thought grounded him to reality.

The sun began to disappear, morphing into the white eye of the penguin he had seen the night before. Gregor shook his thoughts clear and found himself on the Edge, a projection hanging over a small canyon of jagged rocks fifty meters below. He jumped back; another step and he would have fallen to his death.

He heard a terrible scream behind him. He knew what was coming. It was the Skua, come to push him over so it could feed on what remained of his battered body when he fell. There was no time to turn and fight. There was nowhere to run. Death came at him on the wings of a demon. With no other option, Gregor simply fell backward. He felt the stab of the Skua's beak, but his weight was more than the predatory bird could bear. The bird toppled through the air, finally righting itself, and Gregor heard the wings flap away into the night.

He stayed on his back for several moments, catching his breath and shaking off the adrenaline of the experience. He stood, surveying his surroundings, and when he was sure no more shape-shifting shadows were about him, he caught his breath. He looked at the flat slabs of stone where the Court of Sparroth met, and then to the Edge, the place where, when the rare verdict of death was passed, executions were carried out. He shivered at how close he had come being executed by a phantom.

The trek back to the beach was made with as much haste as Gregor could muster. He wanted nothing more to do with mountains for a while. When he reached his nest, he found the Bakorpheous crystal where it had been placed when he'd fallen asleep. He also found Stone exactly as he had last seen him, asleep and making heavy noises through whatever dreams an Elephant Seal had. Gregor gave him a soft peck with his beak. "Wake me the next time I go sleepwalking."

Stone shifted slightly, cracked open one eye, and made a noise that would have been equally at home coming from either end. He closed his eye and was asleep in seconds.

Gregor looked at his friend, envying his slumber. It would be a long while before he'd let himself rest so deeply again.

CHAPTER 10

The morning sun pulled Admiral Gregor from his restless sleep. He'd woken at regular intervals through the remainder of his night, expecting visits from wraiths and demons. When doubt entered his mind, he squeezed close to Stone, deciding to take the chance of having the monstrous bull rolling over on him and smothering him to death was a better alternative than throwing one's self off a cliff while in a dream state. The admiral was pleased that neither came to pass.

Stone sat off to the side, basking in the morning light after his early morning feeding run. Gregor followed his friend's lead and went on a feeding run of his own. After only grabbing a few small fish and a not-so-ripe squid, he gave up on food; he didn't have much of an appetite anyway.

When he returned, he checked on the Bakorpheous crystal, making sure it was where he had left it. He placed it between two small rocks and buried it beneath a recent clump of guano, then looked at it from several angles. Satisfied it was safely stashed, Gregor began a quick and purposeful walk toward Vicar Kaff's grotto.

Gregor arrived to find the shallow cave empty. He walked through the recesses, calling to the vicar. Receiving no reply, he turned to leave but spotted the old piece of wood, half-covered with debris. He looked around for Kaff one more time, and with no sign of him, Gregor let curiosity get the better of him.

He traced lines in the sand with his claws as he stood over the wood, debating whether or not he should lift it or go on his way. After less than a moment of deliberation, he took the old wood in his beak and flipped it over.

Disappointment washed over him when no dazzling array of colored crystals stared back at him. He dug through the sand, only finding a few pieces of dull, clear glass encrusted with dirt. He let out a long breath, flipped the wood slat down, and turned to leave. He jerked to a stop when Kaff spoke.

"It's not polite to rummage through one's nest when they're not there." Kaff sounded anything but threatening. "Did you find what you were looking for?"

"No. Not unless one of your magic talismans can ward off waking dreams." He sounded accusing.

Kaff froze. His eyes went wide, and he stammered for words. "Wh-Whatever do you mean, Admiral? Waking dreams?" He turned watching the broad mouth of the cave.

The vicar *did* know something more; now he was sure of it. "Why don't you answer that question for me, Vicar Kaff? Tell me why I woke last night to find myself standing on the Edge. Tell me why a Skua attacked me once again. Had I not pulled myself from the dream world, I'd be lying in pieces at the bottom of the ravine."

"The Bakorpheous crystal did not protect you?"

"No. Maybe. I don't know. I thought of it just before I came to my senses. So in that manner, it did." Gregor wanted information and felt an urge to throttle the vicar. But he knew Kaff well enough to know he wouldn't divulge what was needed if it came to that. "Will you please tell me what's going on? For two nights I've been pursued by something or someone," he said with forced patience.

"What did you see in the dream?" Kaff asked. His eyes looked haunted, as if seeing a specter from the past.

Gregor explained everything he remembered: the change of night to morning, the shape-shifting shadow, and finally the white-eyed penguin. "It was like he was there but not. But the Skua was very real. I carry a wound to prove it was real."

Kaff examined the evidence, walked away, and returned carrying the bloom of an Alpine Cat's-tail. "Turn around," he said through his clinched beak and shook the thistles over Gregor's injury.

"I don't see how rubbing a flower on me is going to help," Gregor said, twisting his neck, trying to see.

Kaff ignored him and continued, adding a clicking growl to his ritual.

"How does beseeching the Shaper help?" he asked, growing impatient with the vicar.

After another minute of Kaff ignoring him, he ended the rite and placed the pink flower back where he'd found it. "Admiral Gregor, Huhellsus makes the seasons change, and he can heal as well. The act of healing is change. However, in this case we have to go beyond the normal methods of healing."

"By normal, you mean not doing anything at all?"

Kaff gave Gregor a quick glance and began rummaging through another pile of miscellanea. "The *flower*, as you called it, is a rare color. The Ancients give these but once in a season, if that. You're fortunate. When the bloom withers and crumbles, the blessing dies with it. This *flower* was very dry."

"All right, will you tell me why you're using your one magic flower on a simple scratch?"

"It's not a simple scratch," Kaff snapped. He walked outside, with Gregor following, and looked toward the summit of Mount Kraysol. "Chaos dwells in the mountain."

"You speak like chaos is a living thing." Gregor didn't like where this was going. Vicar Kaff spoke of superstitions; what he needed were facts.

"This chaos is neither alive nor dead. If he is the one who visited your dreams, that is. He can't be truly alive."

"Who is this chaos?" Gregor demanded. He had had enough of ghost stories. "Your delusions are wearing thin."

Kaff turned to him. His eyes showed both anger and fear. "The one I speak of is Elatha-Cadail, the demon of dreams and chaos."

"Elatha-Cadail? That old hermit died before I was hatched. I've had enough of this." He clinched his beak and walked away. "When you have anything of use to tell me, you know where to find me."

Kaff called to him. "Admiral, you must learn the story of King Escalefact."

"I know the story, Vicar," Gregor replied. "He died before the hermit."

"King Escalefact walked off the Edge in the night."

Admiral Gregor stopped. A sudden coldness crawled up his body from tail to tip. His breathing became shallow; his heart hammered against his chest. The world seemed to spin as he turned back to face Kaff.

The fright in Vicar Kaff's eyes matched the fear in Gregor's. "Come back inside, and I will tell you what was told to me." He looked at the mountain once more and hurried into his cave.

CHAPTER 11

"Relax, Admiral Gregor. What I have to say might take some time," Kaff said, motioning toward a depression in the ground.

Gregor shook his head, coughing a disbelieving laugh. "You tell me I nearly died the same way as King Escalefact, and you think I can relax? Apparently you never had a demon try to murder you in your sleep."

"Relax your legs, not your mind."

"That's *really* not very reassuring," Gregor said with a touch of humor. He squatted and looked at Vicar Kaff expectantly.

"What I'm to tell you should be kept between us. Most of it is rumor, hearsay… speculation. But as we discussed, all myths have a foundation in reality." Kaff looked at Gregor, waiting for a protest. Receiving none, he swallowed hard and continued. "These stories come to me from Vicar Orn. He was my mentor and very old when I apprenticed to him."

Gregor took a deep breath; Kaff's sermons were always longer than the day, he could imagine how lengthy a story would be.

"In the days of King Escalefact, father to Elinthaw, Elatha-Cadail was the advisor to the throne. He guided him on many issues, including offering advice when dealing with neighboring colonies. Elatha-Cadail, who was once a lord in the Order of Kings, had risen through the ranks quickly, going from a junior member to a full lord in less than two winter's time. Noticing his knowledge of events within the colony were uncanny, the king took him on as his advisor. It was then that Elatha-Cadail began to show his true motives."

"And what were they?" Gregor asked, trying to mask his impatience. He wanted Kaff to get to the point where it mattered to him.

"As I said, he advised the king on dealing with other colonies. Elatha-Cadail wanted Escalefact to go to war against King Rosius's colony to the north. But Escalefact wanted nothing to do with it. It was unheard of at that time. There hadn't been a war since the Great Auk War. When the king refused, Elatha-Cadail attempted a coup, but King Escalefact, as you know, was well loved by the colony, and the coup was thwarted. When Escalefact learned of Elatha-Cadail's role as the instigator, he put him on trial in the Court of Sparroth, and Elatha-Cadail was sentenced to death at the Edge."

"If he was put to death, then we're dealing with somebody else. An impersonator. Nobody can survive a fall from the Edge. The fall is too far; the rocks are too sharp."

Kaff turned away. "I never said he fell. Here is where the details are muddled. Hearsay and rumor govern what I am about to tell you, but it doesn't preclude truth."

Gregor stood and tilted his head. "Does it pertain to my dreams?"

"Yes, Admiral. All of this does. You need to know the whole story."

Gregor hesitated before squatting again. Kaff was as nervous and superstitious of penguin as he had ever known. Even speaking about these things was causing him anxiety. "All right, Vicar. I apologize. Let me hear it all."

Kaff looked at Gregor sideways and nodded. "The story as I learned it tells us that as Elatha-Cadail was being forced to the Edge, a great cacophony of bird calls erupted from the canyon. A cloud of Skua came from the mountain, driving the executioners back and whisking Elatha-Cadail to safety in the mountain."

"You mean in the *mountains*, right? Not in the mountain."

"I meant what I said, Admiral. Now let me continue. I can only say this once. King Escalefact witnessed the escape and called upon his bravest guards. They pursued the Skuas, following them into the caldera of the living mountain. It was there they lost him. The king, with no other explanation available to him, assumed the Skuas carried off Elatha-Cadail and consumed him."

"I'm going to assume he wasn't eaten," Gregor said, stretching.

Kaff ignored him. "Three winters passed and Escalefact's first heir was hatched. But the hunting was sparse that year and, like so many others, he was lost to famine. And so it was for each hatchling of the king and queen. Whether by starvation or predation, his heirs were lost. When bounty returned, Elinthaw was hatched, and the king had his heir once more.

"After his presumed death, tales of Elatha-Cadail arose from the beaches. Mostly fables to frighten misbehaving fledglings, but the legend grew, and like every folktale, they carried an element of truth. Some said that Elatha-Cadail was abandoned after he hatched, that his parents saw the evil within him and left him to his fate. They said the Skuas came to make an easy meal of him. But Elatha-Cadail was born with a gift from Cuasan himself; it was said he could enter one's dream or control the minds of the simple-minded Skuas. And, much like later in his life, he controlled the birds and they carried him to safety, feeding and caring for him until he reached maturity."

"The tales eventually reached the king's ears and became beset with worry. Elatha-Cadail had been a newcomer to the land when he made headway into the Order of Kings; he seemingly possessed the gift of foresight. To make matters worse, Elinthaw soon began having dreams of a penguin with white eyes, the same as you. Escalefact knew something had to be done, lest he lose another hatchling. Ignoring the protests of the queen, he climbed to the summit and stood in the Talon of Wisdom, calling out to Elatha-Cadail, challenging him to show himself and fight in the open. He stood on the mountain for six nights. On the seventh he went home, satisfied that Elatha-Cadail was nothing more than a legend, a story to frighten the gullible. On the morning of the eighth day, King Escalefact's body was found on the rocks below the Edge."

"How does he enter dreams?" Gregor asked, alarmed.

"Vicar Orn once spoke with Lapasia, who at the time was coming into her abilities as an Oracle. She suggested Elatha-Cadail was an Oracle, but, an Oracle can only be female. The power corrupts the minds of males who receive it, and if allowed to reach maturity, he would be something more akin to a demon, the antithesis of what a seer should be. A male Oracle uses the gift of Sight to see into the dream world, not the waking world."

Gregor considered what Kaff had said. He knew very little about oracles. "What happened after Escalefact's death?"

"King Elinthaw's dreams subsided, and, as they always do, the memories of what took place disappeared along with those who carried them. Only the king and I know the story, and now you do as well, Admiral."

Gregor stood and stretched. "If any of these rumors are true, there is no way Elatha-Cadail is behind my dreams. Escalefact died long before I was hatched, which would make this Elatha-Cadail at least forty winters old."

"As I first told you, Admiral Gregor, most of what I know is only hearsay, secondhand knowledge *from* secondhand knowledge. But what you are experiencing is too similar to be coincidental."

Gregor paced the length of the cave. "Then what do you suggest I do?"

Kaff looked at him, his eyes earnest and caring. "Commune with the Ancients. Beseech their protection. Repent, cleanse your spirit, and perhaps they will aid you."

"If Elatha-Cadail really is alive, then he is old, older even than the king." Gregor stopped. Gelika had said Elinthaw had outlived most penguins. "Don't you find it strange, Vicar, that the only survivor connected to your tale is the oldest living king on this island or, for all we know, anywhere?"

Kaff's gaze shifted downward, and he scanned the ground, back and forth. "I… I never really thought about it. What are you suggesting, Admiral?"

"I'm not suggesting anything other than it being an odd coincidence." He went to the cave entrance.

"What are you going to do, Admiral?"

"I'm going to have a talk with the only other one who was there."

CHAPTER 12

The climb to the king's throne seemed more arduous than normal. He hoped it wasn't for nothing. The last he'd seen of Elinthaw, he'd disappeared in the dark.

The first penguin he spotted was Queen Gelika. Her eyes seemed to light up when Gregor approached, but he still had a few things to discuss with her before he would acknowledge the look. As it was, he had to fight to pull his eyes away. He grumbled at seeing her self-satisfied reaction. Gregor kept his feet moving until arriving at the king's court. He was surprised to find several commanders present, headed by Lieutenant Hally.

Hally noticed him. "Admiral Gregor. I didn't expect you. You were less than enthusiastic over the Order's resolution. I half expected you to resign your post."

"I'll resign my post when I reach the Great Sea, *Lieutenant*," he spat, continuing past.

"I'm sorry, Admiral. I see you have yet to be informed. The king has seen me fit to be Vice Admiral. Apparently he sees me as the better fit to lead our warriors to battle."

Gregor kept walking. "Then they're all as good as dead. I've come to see the king, not his remora."

"You might regret your words one day, Admiral," Hally called in a smug, half-amused tone.

"You might regret telling me that, Lieutenant." Gregor climbed the broad natural stairs to the king's dais. There he found Lord Keese and Lordess Tolk in discussion with the king with Lord Chalkfeather. *Great, more of Elinthaw's sycophants*, Gregor thought when saw Chalkfeather. At least Keese was bearable; he didn't know Lordess Tolk to have an opinion. "Your Majesty. I need to speak with you, about… a private matter."

"Ah, Admiral Gregor, you must've heard about Hally's promotion," Elinthaw said, rising quickly. He waved away the members of the Order. "Leave us."

After they left, he turned his attention to Elinthaw. "I couldn't care less about his promotion. If you see him fit to command, then the Taker will have a bountiful gathering."

"Now, Admiral Gregor. Jealousy doesn't become you in the least."

Gregor's head jerked. "Jealousy? I'm sorry, Your Highness, but I am being forthright. Hally is of no concern to me. I've come to discuss much more important matters with you, if you don't mind." He locked eyes with the king. It almost seemed as if Elinthaw was challenging him. The old husk of a penguin wouldn't know what hit him if he did. As Gregor looked in his eyes, something seemed different. He couldn't place it; it just seemed different.

Elinthaw continued his long look at the admiral, finally releasing his gaze, and turning away. "What is it that's so important, Admiral?"

The fact that the king was acting unusually cold toward him didn't escape his notice. Perhaps it had something to do with Hally's promotion and Gregor's apathy toward the matter. He waited a moment longer, trying to gauge what had changed in the king's demeanor. When Elinthaw turned to him, he realized what had changed: his eyes. The cloudiness was gone. He studied them a moment longer to be certain. They were clearer. Gregor took a step back. This wasn't right. But he had come to demand answers, and that's what he'd do. "What can you tell me of Elatha-Cadail? Is he still alive?"

Elinthaw's eyes widened. For moment, Gregor thought they would turn white, and he would find himself in a dream again. They didn't, and the king slumped.

"Elatha-Cadail died many years ago. Now tell me why you want to know." Elinthaw lifted his head.

Gregor stood in wonder. The king seemed to age ten winters in a blink. He looked around; all was as it should be. Not knowing how else to answer him, Gregor lied. "Just old tales, Your Highness. Some of the refugees were talking about an old myth."

Elinthaw appeared to be digesting the lie. "Oh, I see. Elatha-Cadail died long ago, before I was hatched, I believe. He was executed for treason, if I remember my father's stories correctly."

Gregor watched the King for another moment. "I'm sorry to bother you, My King. I thought we might have a threat living among us. I was wrong. They were indeed just old tales. I will take my leave." He bowed and made a motion to leave.

"Admiral," Elinthaw said. "Will you send Queen Gelida to me, please?"

Gregor cleared his throat. "You mean Queen *Gelika,* don't you, Your Highness?"

Elinthaw looked confused. "Oh, yes. Did I say Gelida? She was a remarkable penguin, wasn't she?"

"Yes, Your Highness. I will send Queen Gelika at once." Gregor left.

CHAPTER 13

The wind swept down the mountain, pushing at Admiral Gregor's back, urging him to do what he didn't want to do. He still held no desire to speak with Queen Gelika, even if it was the king's orders.

She stood near the walkway leading to the king's court before the backdrop of a yellow, orange, and violet sunset tinged with streaks of aquamarine and vermillion. The sight made him forget why he was angry with her. He clawed at his memory until he pried it loose. The reason seemed to have lost some its strength. Nevertheless, his animosity persisted. "My Queen, King Elinthaw has asked me to send you to him," he said as he approached.

Gelika stared at him. "You don't trust me, Admiral," she said while he fidgeted.

"You are my queen. I have no choice but to trust you," Gregor said, looking away.

"That's not what I meant." Their eyes met. "Walk with me, Gregor."

"But Elinthaw gave me orders to send you, and there are others watching." He looked toward Hally's group, trying to remain inconspicuous. The group of officers were too busy with proud and boastful proclamations of their military brilliance to pay them any mind.

"I don't care. Let them talk, let the king see…." She looked away and shook her head. "Walk with me, Admiral Gregor."

"Are you sure that's wise?" he asked, glancing at the king's dais.

Her eyes filled with mischief. "I am your queen, Admiral. You must do as I say."

Gregor barked a laugh. "Then my options are limited, lest I be seen as treasonous to the throne."

"Now you're getting it, Admiral," she said, leading him up the trail.

Once they'd gotten far enough away, Gelika squatted and looked toward the darkening horizon. Gregor sat next to her and watched the night consume the day.

They sat in silence for several minutes before Gelika spoke. "I have never known freedom. The choices of my life were made before I even knew I had any. My coat was still brown when I was chosen to be pair-bonded with Elinthaw. Being young, I didn't know any different. I thought it was how things were."

"It should never be that way," Gregor said, not taking his eyes from the horizon.

Gelika nodded slightly. "Do you remember our adventures before we lost our browns? It was like that thick fuzzy down not only sheltered us from the cold but from life's harsh reality as well."

"Plenty of brown-coats were taken during that time; they weren't sheltered from a harsh reality."

"I do love the way you take a fond memory and turn it into a reminder of life's struggles," she said with a breathy laugh.

Gregor stiffened. Here she was, the queen, telling him of a cherished time in her life, and he had turned it into a grizzly reminder of dying fledglings. *What am I doing?* He cleared his throat. "No, no. It's just that I, I...." He took a breath. "I do remember. How could I forget?"

She looked at him. "I remember too. I remember when we returned from the sea for the season and being taken to the king's court, and watching you as I was led up this hill. I remember wanting nothing more than to stay on the beach, to share more adventures, share a lifetime of adventures with you. But instead I became the queen, sentenced to spend a lifetime pair-bonded to a penguin so old, the mountains look young by comparison."

Gregor stood. "Then why wait until now? We've seen one another a multitude of times, and only recently have you shown you even remembered me."

Gelika motioned for him to sit. She continued when he did as she'd asked. "The next season Gelida was hatched. A winter after that, before she had matured, our parents were taken. In most cases browns are left to fend for themselves, and usually they die. But I saved her. I brought her here, saw her to maturity, perhaps hoping I would have a friend. Soon after, she changed. She went from being a quiet sister to a proud rival. Elinthaw and I despised each other at first sight, but it was different for them. She said the things he wanted to hear. When I opposed allying with the Overlord, she encouraged him. When I urged us not to attack the men here, she assured him it was the right decision. She seemed to take pleasure in guiding him into poor choices, and it cost her her life."

"A lot paid for these choices. I fear that men will return. I've heard stories of what they are capable of. Countless penguins were killed in moments from their weapons. Once they learn of what took place here, our fate will be sealed."

"For once your pessimism might be well-founded."

"Observing reality isn't pessimistic," Gregor replied, feeling morose after hearing what he'd missed. He let the silence linger for a while, until he'd built up enough courage to say what he felt. "You weren't the only one who watched that day. I didn't know why you left. I thought it was your choice. I thought that until a few winters ago."

"How could I tell you?"

"You couldn't," Gregor said after a long breath. His suspicions rose. He decided it was time to ask the hard questions, even if it meant killing what had begun. "Are you saying this so I will assist you in pushing Elinthaw to relinquish the throne?"

Gelika stared at Gregor, letting the silence hang until it felt like a physical thing. "Gregor, I would do this alone or stay where I am until I am called to the Great Sea, if only to prove to you I'm not."

The last hints of daylight vanished into the sea. Gregor stood and looked for the moon, which had yet to arrive. His eyes followed her as she stood and moved toward him. "Regardless of the outcome, we can never be more than what we are. If I assist you, or if I stand by the wayside, your name will be dishonored. They'll say we were in collusion. We would have to stay in the shadows."

"Are you so above reproach, you cannot see yourself as my paramour until the time comes for me to step down?"

Gregor turned away. "And when will that be?" he asked, watching the ground.

"I can't say with certainty." Gelika stepped around to face him. "I know of your emptiness, Gregor. It doesn't have to be that way."

He lifted his head. "What good could come of this?"

"More than you know."

^^^

Vice Admiral Hally crept to the rear of the dais, took a satisfied breath, and rapped his beak on an old plank of ship wood. King Elinthaw snapped his eyes open, jerking out of his slumber. Hally stepped back and examined the king until he was sure the old penguin was actually awake.

"What is it? Who's there?" Elinthaw said with an old, cracking voice.

Vice Admiral Hally bowed. "I apologize, You Highness. It is I, your commander. I come with important information." He watched the king, making certain the old penguin had actually awoken.

"What is it, Vice Admiral? I'm old and need my sleep."

"Again, I apologize. There is something you must know about the queen."

Elinthaw stood on shaky legs. "Get on with it, Hally."

"The queen was seen consorting with Admiral Gregor. That was why she didn't come when summoned." Hally kept his head bowed, trying to show humility before the king.

Elinthaw seemed to mull it over; gray eyes scanned the night appearing to search for answers. He found Hally, clicked his beak, and brought the vice admiral to attention. "I am going on leave again. Have Gelika brought to the Court of Sparroth. Have the charges brought before the tribunal, and have her put to the Edge until I return to render the final verdict."

"Your command is my desire, Your Majesty. And what of Admiral Gregor?"

"I will deal with the admiral in my own time. Prepare yourself for your promotion, Admiral Hally." Elinthaw left, making his way up Mount Kraysol at once.

Hally watched the King leave and let out a satisfied breath.

CHAPTER 14

The morning sun seemed to increase the gloom near the caldera, magnifying a hazy glow within the fog. The mist dampened sights and sounds, confusing King Elinthaw's senses as he skirted the edge. Carried on legs tired with age, the king pressed forward, stumbling on loose rocks and slipping in the ashy mud. The entrance of the cave presented itself through the miasma, bleak, cold, yet familiar and inviting. Elinthaw sat at the mouth, watching the condensation run along tiny crevasses until escape was found, and it dripped into a murky puddle at his feet. He waited for what would come, for what always came when he became weak.

He closed his eyes. The silence was total, the mist nearly quieting the sound of his breathing. A distant call pried his eyes open. He waited, and the call grew louder. The call turned shrill, a grating cackle echoing through the cave, growing closer by the second. Elinthaw braced himself. The Skua flew from the maw, nearly knocking him to the ground. It was time.

The king entered the cave, and the mist followed. He stumbled and slipped until he reached a small stalagmite, dripping with moisture, iridescent and calcified, reflecting light from an unseen fissure.

A terrible whisper, sounding like claws scratching on rock, seeped from the darkness. "You have come before your time, Elinthaw. I don't appreciate my followers growing too needy."

Elinthaw scanned the gloom, looking for the source of the whisper. Unable to find its owner, he lowered his head. "Admiral Gregor came to me. He asked about Elatha-Cadail, and my mind grew foggy."

"Gregor is a problem we will soon be rid of. He will fall to the Nocturemortis, the same as Escalefact."

"Hally has informed me the queen and Gregor are in league against me. I've ordered Gelika to stand trial and placed on the Edge."

"Then your troubles are nearly over. The queen will die, and her supporters will follow or flee."

"But she is the sister of Gelida. I can't put her to death, if only for her sister's sake."

"Your weakness sickens me." The voice transformed from a scratching whisper to a grinding echo. "Gelika is the cause of Gelida's death, and you shy away from having her executed."

Elinthaw shook his head. "I am the cause of Gelida's death. It was my foolish alliance with Antaean. Had I not chosen to go to war; had I had the foreknowledge of what was to come, she would still be alive."

A shadow cut through the mist so fast, Elinthaw had no chance to brace himself. It struck him with enough force to send him flailing through the air on a collision course with the cave wall. The impact stole his breath and threatened to steal his consciousness. He stood, the world swirling around him.

"Idiot! You believe that only to deny the truth," the voice thundered, eliciting an answering call from the Skua in the distance. "Gelika convinced her sister to insist you go to war, knowing she would lead the attack to impress you. Gelika knew of the futility of the attack and stayed behind. She knew of your affinity for Gelida. Her jealousy turned her against you, and now she and Admiral Gregor are conspiring to murder you. Yet still you sit, wallowing in self-pity. Be strong. For once in your life, surpass your father. Have the queen executed, move against the alliance and the Royal Emperors, and finish what was started by the Council of Thrace. You will be exalted by all, and the Kings will assume their rightful spot as sovereigns of the oceans."

The Skua soared through the tunnel, knocking Elinthaw back down. It stood on the king's chest, pinning him to the ground, paralyzing him through fear. The shadow circled him, stopping on the border between form and vapor. White eyes appeared within the apparition. A sickly smell filled the cavern, and the mountain seemed to growl. Elinthaw wanted to close his eyes but couldn't.

"Kill her. Have her executed tomorrow. She forced her way onto the throne, preventing you from having your true queen. Kill her, and you will live another winter."

Elinthaw turned away. A moment later, he nodded. The white eyes dimmed, and the Skua took flight. The king walked out of the cave, hopping over obstacles, his legs strong and his mind sharp.

CHAPTER 15

Queen Gelika walked to her nest at sunrise, stopping to stare at the crepuscular rays of dawn creeping over the mountaintops and cutting their way through the low clouds. The world would be different now. She would soon be free of Elinthaw and the lifetime of emptiness. Whether she continued to rule in his place or if another leader was found mattered very little to her; the colony would be better off without the king leading them into extinction. She took a long breath; the end was finally in sight.

Her calm crashed against the rocks when she heard Hally, near the King's court, telling her to halt. Of all of Elinthaw's advisors and sycophants, she despised Hally the most. He would trample his own egg if the king so much as hinted at it, and his arrogance was excessive even for a King Penguin. What the toady wanted at this time of day was beyond her. She hoped it would be brief.

"Enjoying the morning breeze, Gelika?" he asked.

Something in his voice set off alarms in Gelika's head. "That's Queen Gelika to you, Lieutenant."

"That's Vice Admiral to you, Gelika."

"I am the queen, and you will address me as such or be put to sea. And I will address you as I please. When you become fit to wear the title of vice admiral, I will address you as such, but I do not foresee a time when that shall be. Now go away before I lose my patience."

"I'm sorry. I forgot to make myself clear. You no longer have authority as the queen. King Elinthaw has issued a warrant for you to stand trial for treason against the throne. You are to be taken to the Edge at once to await the king's judgement."

Hally stood in front of her with a sickening smugness in his eyes she wanted to slap off his face. So she did. The slap put the vice admiral on the ground in a heartbeat. "I've warned you once, and that is all you will get. Try to stop me again, and you'll receive much worse. Now where is the king? I want to hear this from him, not his lackey."

Hally rose, ready to strike. The warning in the queen's eyes made him hesitate. "The king has sought communion with the Ancients. He will render his judgement when he returns."

"Then be on your way," Gelika said, pushing Hally aside once more.

He rushed toward Gelika, knocking her against the step of the king's court. "You are under arrest. Resist further, and you will be punished before the king finds you guilty." He looked past her. "Guards, assist me in subduing this criminal."

The queen slapped him aside once again and faced the guards, who approached her with caution, their doubt obvious in their movements. She was going to meet them when she felt a searing pain in her back. She spun around to find Hally glaring at her, blood dripping from his beak.

"I warned you. And this is your final warning. Surrender to the Court of Sparroth."

"You don't have the strength to take me," Gelika growled.

The guards closed in and overpowered the queen. She fought as well as she could, but in the end, she was overcome.

"You're right, my former queen. I don't have the strength, but my guards do." Hally looked at the captain of the guard. "Take her to the Edge and hold her there."

CHAPTER 16

Captain Thane hurried up Mount Kraysol to the Court of Sparroth, trailed by Vicar Kaff. "Why in the world would Lieutenant Hally put the queen on trial? I swear, if this is some sort of power play by him, I'll break his beak in two. I don't care what his position is with the King."

"Putting yourself in the same position as the queen would only serve to make matters worse, Captain Thane. We mustn't jump to conclusions. I'm certain this is all a misunderstanding." Kaff wheezed, trying to keep up with her.

The two arrived and headed straight for the Edge. They spotted Queen Gelika behind four stout guards who stood shoulder to shoulder on the outcropping of rock, forming a picket that prevented her from getting past. Her only way to leave was down. If the king found her guilty, others would join the picket and march forward until the convicted was forced over and dashed against the jagged rocks far below. Thane would not let that happen regardless of the king's verdict.

Captain Thane leaned into the vicar. "Kaff, I need you to go to Admiral Gregor at once. Tell him the queen is slated for execution. He's our only hope to save her. Go now."

"But you don't know what the verdict will be. Perhaps the king is just giving her a public reprimand for her friendship with Admiral Gregor."

"Do you really believe that? Look at what you see. Most of the Order is here. The King's guards and Hally standing on that rock, just begging to be knocked off and pecked, and trampled and slapped and—"

"I get the idea, Captain." Kaff interrupted. "But I can't go. I am required to be present for trials. It is an obligation that cannot be shirked. The execution cannot take place without a vicar present. You should go."

Thane stared at Kaff for several heartbeats. "If the execution can't happen without your presence, why are you still here and not getting help?"

Kaff opened his beak to explain his duty when her words caught up with him. "Ah. I see your point, Captain Thane."

A chorus of calls erupted in the distance.

"Hurry! The herald just announced his arrival. Go, go, go. Don't stop for any reason."

He rushed off, back the way they had come.

King Elinthaw strolled to the center of a stone clearing. With no further preamble, Vice Admiral Hally stepped in front of the crowd. "Speak the charges," the king said, his voice full of strength.

Hally did a small double take at hearing the command in the king's voice. He straightened, puffing his chest. "Gelika, the queen, has been charged with treason against the throne, instigating rebellion, breaking vows with the king, and intent to cause mayhem."

Thane looked to Gelika, trying to reassure her. Instead of finding worry on the face of the queen, she saw bemusement mixed with smoldering contempt. Her eye caught Thane's. "Intent to cause mayhem?" the captain asked.

Gelika shrugged.

"What valid witnesses do you have to reinforce these very serious claims?" King Elinthaw asked.

"A member of the Order of Kings has come forward to bear witness against the queen," Hally replied.

A murmur swept through the mass of penguins. Captain Thane

scanned the crowd and spotted Lordess Tolk. She watched her look at the others until Thane's gaze met Tolk's wide and scared eyes. *Betrayed*, Thane thought. She thought the refugee would've appreciated her status in a colony which had taken her in.

"Call the witness," Elinthaw bellowed.

Hally faced the multitude. "I call Lord Keese as witness before the king."

Thane looked at Tolk, who was slowly backing away from the crowd. Next she looked at Gelika, who paid her no mind, choosing instead to focus her glare on the corpulent Lord Keese. The captain pushed her way to Tolk.

"What do we do?" Tolk asked, her voice trembling with fear.

"You have to go," Thane told her. She knew she would have to follow, but she wouldn't leave the queen until help arrived. She heard Lord Keese's proclamations in the background, naming Tolk and Thane as part of the conspiracy against the king. She ignored the ruckus. "Go to Talon of Wisdom. There's a path on the far side of the summit. It's a dangerous climb, but it's better than waiting for them to arrest you. There's a small depression in the cliff about seventy steps down. Hide there and wait. We'll come for you."

"What are you going to do?" Tolk asked before leaving.

Thane looked at Gelika. "I'm going to slap a few heads and then get myself arrested."

"What? You can't throw your life away. We need to leave—"

"Trust me. Everything will be fine. But you need to go now."

Lordess Tolk hesitated but thought better of it when she heard Hally call for the arrest of Captain Thane.

"There she is," a voice called from the crowd.

A group of soldiers ran toward Captain Thane and skidded to a stop, facing them. The group nervously looked between them. "Who's first? Which of you has the nerve to arrest your captain?"

"What are you doing? Arrest her," Hally said from the background.

"Well? Are you going to stand there wasting daylight or arrest me?" Thane asked.

The first soldier stepped forward. "Captain Thane, by order of the—"

Thane spun and slapped the soldier. "That's for thinking you could," she spat and then looked at the others. "Next."

Two more came at her. She met the first with two vicious slaps and rammed her head under the beak of the next, rendering him unconscious in a blink. "That's for even thinking about it." The first of the two soldiers began to get to his feet. She unleashed a flurry of slaps, and the soldier went down again. "And that's for being stupid enough not to stay down."

She raised her flippers. "Do you have any strength beneath your undercoat, or do I have to arrest myself?"

The remaining soldiers looked at one another and rushed forward.

Captain Thane beat them without mercy, slapping one so hard he stood staring blankly at nothing, unconscious on his feet. She continued to slap each one into submission until a dozen soldiers came at her at once, finally subduing her against the rocky ground. "You fight like castrated fledglings. Honestly," she said beneath the weight of them.

They got to their feet and pressed against Thane, keeping her flippers pinned to her side as they slowly walked forward. The huddle eventually arrived before King Elinthaw, who stared down at the group from his position on the stone slab.

"You have been charged with conspiracy to commit treason against the throne. How do you plead?"

"What evidence do you have other than your addled and paranoid mind, and a fat tail-sniffer who would say anything to become less than useless?" Thane snapped.

"Guilty," Elinthaw said, devoid of emotion. "Take her to the Edge."

Hally moved ahead of the huddle, leading them to the Edge.

"That was some fight, wasn't it, Hally? Oh wait, you weren't there. You were back here, shaking in your feathers, suckling the king like a seal pup at its mother's teat."

"I'm going to enjoy watching you fall to your death. The colony will be a much better group without you," Hally said, keeping his eyes forward.

"You know, if I ever get hold of you, I'm going to snap your neck and shove your head so far up your squidhole, the last thing you'll ever see is what you ate for supper." The guard closest to her suppressed a laugh. She looked at him. "That was good, huh? I don't know how I'd pull it off, but it'd be fun trying."

"Then it's a good thing for me you'll be dead, Captain Thane. Put her with the queen," Hally barked. The escort slowly parted, the rear guard walking forward, forcing her to the outcropping.

"Hello, Queen," Thane said.

"Captain, good of you to join me. Are we getting out of this?" Gelika said.

"You bet we are," Thane answered, looking at the guard standing directly in front of her.

"And how will we accomplish this escape?"

"I don't know yet." Thane said. King Elinthaw began to speak, and she redirected her attention to him.

"Gelika and Thane. You have been found guilty on all charges. The penalty is death. Do you have any last requests?"

"Yeah," Thane said. "Pull Hally's head out of your crap shooter. He wanted to see this."

King Elinthaw had no reaction. "Vicar Kaff, speak the final blessing so we can be done with this."

Hally looked around when no reply came. "Vicar Kaff, the king gave you a direct order." He continued to scan the audience. "Where is Vicar Kaff?"

Thane leaned into Gelika. "And there's the first part to us getting out of here."

CHAPTER 17

Kaff slowed his pace travelling down the mountain. Each time he tried to run, forward momentum became too much to bear, and he planted himself into the ground. After the fifth attempt, and swearing he had scraped the last feather from his chest, he decided prudence should hold sway over his descent, and walking best served prudence.

He traversed the sloping hills with more speed until he reached the beach where the Elephant Seals and Admiral Gregor nested. He walked across the loose sand, careful to avoid any seals. He scanned the sparse landscape until he saw a large boulder, out of place on the flat beach. He knew in an instant he had at least found Stone.

Kaff stumbled and tripped in his haste to find Gregor. When he drew near the huge bull, he pulled back. He wasn't sure if the monstrosity would accept newcomers. He carefully circumnavigated the beast until he spotted what could only be Gregor's nesting place. The ground crunched beneath his feet, sounding like thunderclaps in his ears. He didn't want to startle Stone awake. When he arrived at the nest without invoking the bull's wrath, he spoke a quiet invocation to the Ancients and cleared his throat. "You are Stone, friend of Gregor?"

Stone was silent and still.

"Please, if you understand me, can you indicate where Admiral Gregor is? His friends are in danger. They need his help." Kaff waited for some sort of response, or at least an acknowledgement the Elephant Seal was aware of his presence. Receiving none, he crept closer.

He approached Stone's massive head, marveling at its size. The long, bulbous nose growled with each breath. "Stone, I need your help. Do you understand what I'm saying? I'm trying to find Gregor." He leaned forward until his beak was inches away from the enormous nose.

Stone lifted his head in a flash and let out an offensive-sounding snort. Kaff screamed, back-peddled, and fell on his back. The bull rolled to his side, making trumpeting, flatulent noises and scratching his stomach before laying down and closing his eyes.

The vicar's heart raced as he tried to catch his breath. "You did that on purpose," he accused. After taking a full minute to regain his composure, Kaff approached Stone once more. "Did you hear what I asked you? Did you understand?"

Stone honked a fart.

"Some help you are. I guess I'm on my own." Kaff walked to the where the sea rolled to a stop at his feet, looking across the endless surface. He looked across the beach, noticing the relative quiet of the neighboring penguins. He decided Gregor must be on his feeding run and walked into the waves, continuing his search.

Buffeted by the surf, Kaff tumbled back to the shore. Never being more than an average swimmer for a penguin, he redoubled his resolve and broke through the heavier waves. He scanned the water, picking up the dark silhouettes of hunting Kings. He swam to each group he spotted, hoping to find Gregor. He stopped a passing penguin, motioning for him to surface. "Have you seen Admiral Gregor? I must find him, it's very important." He knew he was running out of time. King Elinthaw's patience would only last so long before he would decide to circumnavigate tradition.

The other penguin thought about the question far too long. "Yeah I saw him. He's deep hunting today. The shallows have been a little sparse lately."

He dipped below the surface before Kaff could ask him more. There was little else he could do. Gregor could be anywhere, and it would be impossible for him to spot him from above. He decided to go back and try to talk reason to King Elinthaw. He was heading back to shore when a very large object swam past him at such speed, it sent Kaff spinning. He tried to catch sight of what had nearly spun him into the seabed, but it was already long out of sight. He thanked the Ancients it hadn't been a predator.

He swam back to land, doing his best to come up with a strategy to change the king's mind. He could cite the Ancients and the blessings one received through forgiveness, but he was rather certain Hally would throttle him for delaying the execution. As he wracked his brain, the large object swam past him again, this time sending Kaff into a wave which caused him to roll along the seafloor until he was unceremoniously deposited on the shore. Stunned, he stayed on his back until the world stopped spinning enough for him to open his eyes. He let out a startled gasp when Stone's wet nose slapped him in the face, then emitted another disgusting noise.

Vicar Kaff rolled over to get to his feet and saw Admiral Gregor standing over him. "Thank the Ancients," Kaff shouted. "I thought I'd never find you."

Gregor looked at him. "Stone found me. So what is the problem?"

Kaff quickly got to is feet. "The queen. King Elinthaw has her on the Edge. He's going to execute her for treason and her *friendship* with you. Something must be done."

"Thank you, Stone. You did great." Gregor scratched his friend's neck with his beak. Stone honked, followed by a squeak, and undulated away. "Who do we have to help?"

"Captain Thane. That's all I know of."

"Well, she counts for at least a dozen." Gregor stared at the mountain, then snapped toward Kaff. "Vicar, I need you to do something."

"I assure you, Admiral, my value in a fight would put us in the negative."

"You don't have to raise a flipper."

"Sounds like my kind of work."

Gregor fell in step with Kaff. "When I reach the base of the mountain, you call an alarm."

"What sort of alarm?" Kaff asked, sounding skeptical.

"I don't know. Any alarm that will get the Vice Admiral and others off that mountain. Say the humans have returned. Or better yet, say the Royal Emperors have arrived with a full regiment. That'll get their attention."

"You want me to lie, Admiral?"

Gregor lowered his head. "It's either that or let the Queen and possibly Thane and myself die."

"But, but, I'm a current to the Ancients."

"You can repent later. I'm sure Huhellsus will understand."

"I wouldn't repent to Huhellsus, Admiral. My sermons surely must've taught you that by now."

"Just do it, Vicar. It's our only chance, and I'm not even sure it's a good chance. I have to go." Gregor went off at a quick pace. "And come to the court after you call. I might need help."

Kaff stared after Gregor. It was all becoming too much. The return of the demon, a vicar purposely lying, the king executing his queen—all of this in a matter of days. "Chaos has come indeed." The admiral's form grew smaller as he rushed to save the queen. Kaff let out a heavy breath and walked toward the water.

CHAPTER 18

"There's no sign of Vicar Kaff, Your Majesty. It's possible he might not have received the message." Hally swiveled his head, hoping to catch sight of the coward.

King Elinthaw stepped down from his dais. "No, Vice Admiral. He is in collusion with the usurpers. When he is found, he will join the others below the Edge. We will proceed without him."

"I understand your impatience, Your Highness. But what will the masses think if we break from protocol? It could inspire some half-cocked idea that Gelika was a martyr or worse."

"Did I say this was open for discussion? Do as I've ordered, or I will find another who is more willing."

Hally took a step back. He had seen Elinthaw upset in the past, but the king's renewed vigor and barely contained anger frightened him. Regardless, he was just as anxious to be rid of Thane as the king was to be rid of Gelika. "Begin the execution," Hally cried.

The milling crowd went silent. The guards clicked to one another and the order to move forward came from the commander. The executioners stepped toward the Edge in perfect sync, pushing Thane and Gelika closer to death.

A grating call echoed up the mountainside. Hally ignored it, focusing instead on Thane's smug face as it lost some of its confidence. The call came again, and Hally continued to disregard it until Elinthaw's voice at his back caused him to jump.

"I grow tired of seeing you not perform your duties, Hally. Did you hear the alarm? The Royals have arrived, and we have been caught unaware."

"Your Highness, I'm sure it is only a ruse. Probably one of the Thane's minions creating a distraction or some other nonsense." Hally waited for the king to respond, but the look in Elinthaw's eyes told him he didn't agree with his assessment.

"Look to the beach," Elinthaw said in a tone devoid of any emotion other than hatred. "The browns have gone to safety, and the shoreline is empty. "Do you think Thane could muster such a ruse?"

"I agree, Your Highness," Thane said from the other side of the marching picket. "Let me out of here so I can give the Royals what-for. You can kill me later; let me kill some Royals now."

Hally shot her a look, and Elinthaw ignored her completely.

"Muster the forces. We will meet them on the shore as they come from the surf and watch the tide run red from their blood."

"As you wish, Your Majesty. However, Admiral Gregor is still the acting commander. I doubt the militia will answer my call without his approval." Hally bowed his head, expecting another reprimand.

Elinthaw growled. "As sovereign commander of the Colony of Elinthaw, you are now to assume the position of Grand Admiral."

The necessary announcements were made, ensuring all would eventually receive the proclamation. Grand Admiral Hally turned to Thane with arrogance and disdain. "Captain Thane, I do admit your skills as a fighter and a leader are impressive. If you will vow yourself loyal to the king and myself, I would be happy to grant you a stay of execution."

"I'd as soon jump off a cliff," Thane spat. "Which is what will happen here very shortly."

Hally's laugh was as insincere as it was cold. "As I expected. Enjoy your time in the Great Sea, Captain." He took the commander of the guard aside. "Hold off on the execution until we return. I'm sure we'll be back before the midday. I seriously doubt the Royals have come to our island."

After the entourage left, the Lords of the Order were left standing alone. Captain Thane spotted Lord Keese and pointed him out to Gelika. "Keese," Thane shouted. "I'm coming after you. You know this, right?"

Staying a good distance away, Keese nervously looked at the two prisoners he'd helped convict. "I doubt you'll be in any condition to go after anyone, Lordess Thane," he said, trying to put on a show of bravado for the other members of the Order of Kings.

"Doubt? Do you have any doubt this wasn't part of our plan to lure any traitors to our cause?" Gelika said, surprising Captain Thane.

Lord Keese's beak parted as if to say something. He looked at the others for support, all of whom ignored him and kept on their way. He shuffled away as quickly as he could, looking back and stumbling as he left.

"We'll be seeing you soon, Lord Keese," Thane called after him. She shared a laugh with the queen at seeing Keese run away. "That was good, Gelika. I wish I'd thought of that one."

"We need to expunge the Order and start anew," the queen said, looking at the nearest guard. "Don't you think?"

The guard shifted his eyes, not sure if he should answer.

"But now we wait." Queen Gelika stretched her neck, looking to see if Gregor was close yet.

CHAPTER 19

Admiral Gregor backed into a crevasse, trying to stay hidden when several soldiers, led by the king, passed by. He spied on Elinthaw from his nook. The manner in which the king traversed the uneven landscape was odd. He hopped over rocks and deftly cross a gully as if he had just lost his brown coat. Hally came running up behind, fighting to keep his balance while trying to keep up with Elinthaw. Something was definitely amiss. Gregor had seen signs before but never so strong and overt. The king was older than dirt and here he was, acting like a fledgling.

Once the company passed, he dashed out of his hiding place as fast a penguin could dash. He slipped on loose gravel and tripped over the uneven ground but didn't let it slow him down. He knew he would have little time before the king realized he had been tricked. Coming to a bend, Gregor paused, not wanting to jump out in front of someone he didn't want to see. It turned out his caution was well founded when he heard the heavy breathing of Lord Keese. He pressed against a jut of rock, just out of sight.

The contingent of lords and lordesses passed by not more than a flipper's length away. Gregor never worried; with the exception of Thane and Tolk, the members of the Order never looked past the tip of their own beak. He stared at their backs with contempt. When had the Order of Kings become so weak? They were nothing more than a collective of malfeasant adulators, crapulent on their own sense of vainglorious preeminence. A change needed to be made, and he was certain he wasn't the only penguin who felt that way.

He continued up the path, beginning to tire. He went from the hunt to scaling a mountainside before he knew what he was doing. The Court of Sparroth was in sight, but he needed a moment to catch his breath. He didn't know what he would face once he got there, nor did he know what he'd do once he saved the queen. He did know he'd need his strength. The nearest hillside invited him to lean back for a minute to recharge his energy.

Gregor took several deep breaths, urging his body back to fighting form. He closed his eyes and heard his name called, carried on the wind from someplace far away. He sprang to his feet, wondering if had been caught up in the dream world again. Everything seemed as it should be. The sky was the same, the clouds were moving at normal speed, and even the sun was in the same position. He dismissed it as hearing things and started on his way to the Edge.

He heard his name again, long and drawn out but closer than before. A chill crawled up his back. This time, he'd be ready for whatever he faced. Gregor braced for what was to come.

"Admiral Gregor." The words were terse, with a heavy dose of fear and frustration.

"Vicar Kaff. For a moment I thought I heard the demon in your voice. You're lucky I didn't set an ambush."

Kaff waddled up the path, gasping for breath. "Please don't say things like that, Admiral. Speaking something can sometimes make it real."

"If that's the case, Vicar, then you've brought the Royals down upon us."

"That's not funny."

"Neither is seeing a thousand Royals coming ashore," Gregor said, motioning toward the beach in the distance.

"What?" Kaff cried in alarm, snapping his head toward the coast.

"Now that was funny," Gregor said with a laugh. "Speaking something into existence. There'd be penguins on the moon if that were the case."

"That still wasn't funny, Admiral. And what makes you think there are no penguins on the moon? How would we know if one did speak it into reality?"

"Let's hope there's an ocean up there then," he said, starting to move again.

"What's your plan?" Vicar Kaff asked, looking up the trail.

"I'll know when we get there."

They hurried the rest of the way, coming to a stop just outside the courtyard. The pair hunkered down behind a large rock, and Gregor surveyed the area, searching for threats. "There only seems to be the guards here. Probably making sure Gelika doesn't escape."

"All right. Now that we're here, what's your plan? How are you going to get the queen to safety?"

"That depends on you, Vicar."

"What? What?" Kaff cried in alarm. "How could I possibly win the queen's freedom?"

"Your faith will win her freedom. Let's go, we're running out of time." Gregor stood, not listening to Kaff's protest.

Admiral Gregor boldly strode across the courtyard, approaching the picket of executioners. He tried to hide his surprise when he saw Captain Thane in the same precarious situation as Gelika. "Stand down. The king has acted illegally," Gregor said, putting every bit of authority he could into the command.

"Admiral Gregor," one said nervously. "I'm sorry, but these are the king's orders."

"I understand, but as I said, the king has acted illegally in convicting the queen *and* Captain Thane," he said, giving Thane a questioning look. She responded with a shrug.

The captain of the guard stepped forward, leaving the picket behind him. "Admiral Gregor, with all due respect, you have no authority in these matters. King Elinthaw's words are law. We cannot choose which laws are obeyed and ignored."

"I understand what you said, Captain." Gregor tried to mask his impatience. He knew the king would be approaching the beach soon. "Actually, Captain, you can choose. Vicar Kaff will explain the price you pay in the Great Sea for carrying out the orders of tyranny. Vicar?" he said.

"But, Admiral, in all my studies under Orn, I don't recall ever hearing about—"

Gregor gave him a wide-eyed look, and Kaff took the hint.

Kaff looked at the guards. "I don't recall ever hearing about one who did not suffer mightily for carrying out the orders of a tyrant. In the time of the Ancients, before the story of Calophus, there was a soldier in the army of Cuasan. Cuasan had yet to be cursed, but his path had already been etched in the ice of Neverthaw, the realm of Huhellsus. The soldier, whom we know as… Thakor, was a proud captain. Whatever Cuasan commanded, Thakor would follow his orders without deviation. On the eighth tide of the seventh moon, Cuasan demanded Thakor to take his soldiers and destroy the nest of Miaska, before she took the mantle of the Taker. But Thakor had a deep love for Miaska, and he begged Cuasan to choose another target, anyone other than Miaska, for Thakor and Miaska had paired, and their egg would soon hatch. Cuasan grew angry and demanded Thakor choose. If he sent his soldiers to destroy the nest, he would lose his hatchling and the love of Miaska."

Gelika and Thane listened to the story from behind the picket, taking small steps, moving close to the guards who had turned their backs on them to hear Vicar Kaff's story.

Gregor moved behind the captain and Kaff raised his voice, continuing the tale. "If he chose to defy Cuasan, another would go in his place, his egg would be smashed, and Miaska would still despise him, plus Cuasan would put him to death. Either way, he would lose all and end up in the Dark Sea, where the Great Giver cast all who were seen as evildoers in those times before Cayaske, the land of endless beach."

"It sounds like he was in a no-win situation," one of the guards said.

Kaff nodded. "As often is the case when you turn your back on your conscience. But Thakor had a way out. Cuasan was arrogant. He believed no one could or would oppose his will. His arrogance blinded him to the possibility of disobedience within his ranks. But Thakor, caught in the eddies of fear, failed to see the weakness within Cuasan. In the end, he chose to stand and watch as Cuasan's minions overran the nest. Miaska rose and battled Cuasan, driving him back to where he had come from, but her egg was destroyed. She found Thakor staring into the sun, wishing for blindness so he would not have to see his destroyed egg. Miaska laid a fragment of the shell at his feet. When he looked at her to beg forgiveness, she took his life. On his journey to the Dark Sea, the Great Giver came to Thakor, and he thought he had been saved. But the Great Giver told him those who disobey the good conscience he had put in all penguins, and do nothing to stand against tyranny, are more despised than even those who are the tyrants. Thakor was cast into the Dark Sea, where no light can shine, blind but with sight, with the last image he saw in life etched into his mind's eye so it would be all he would see for all eternity: the sight of his egg destroyed, a constant reminder he'd done nothing to prevent its destruction."

"That's a fine story, Vicar," the captain said. "But old tales will do nothing prevent the king's wrath."

"Then I shall leave you to your damnation." Kaff stepped back, lowering his head.

"What would you have us do, Vicar?" the guard nearest Thane asked.

"Repent!" Captain Thane shouted. The guard turned to her and was met with a head-butt, followed by a slap, which sent him face-first to the ground. "Do as your brother—fall to your stomachs and beg forgiveness!" She unleashed a barrage of slaps on each penguin near her.

Gelika followed the captain's lead and struck the nearest guard. The guard gave a weak slap back. "How dare you strike the queen," she said and unleashed her flurry of slaps on the hapless guard.

"Push them off the Edge," the captain of the guard cried, marching to join the fray.

"That was a mistake, Captain," Gregor said behind him. He rammed the other in his midsection, driving him to the ground, and slapped him repeatedly, giving him no chance to stand.

"Repent, evildoers. Repent," Thane shouted, slapping each guard in a wild frenzy. She pushed forward, trying to break through the picket. The queen threw her weight against Captain Thane's back, and the pair broke through the defenses.

Gregor's victim attempted to stand, but the admiral was on him in a blink, slapping the captain of the guard senseless. When he was sure he wouldn't stand again, he turned his attention to helping Thane and Gelika. He slammed one combatant bodily against a nearby rock and jabbed and pecked at another until the guard threw up his flippers and fled.

Two remained, mesmerized by the ferocity of Captain Thane's attack on one of their own. When she completed brutalizing her latest unfortunate, she looked at the two watching. "Give up your evil ways, lest you be cast to the dunes of Cayaske, forced to wander the land of endless beach, where your body will thirst for the sea but never be quenched."

The remaining guards turned and fled, desperately trying to escape the madness that was Thane.

"Come back and receive your throttling. Only then can you repent." She made a motion to give chase but stopped.

Gregor shook his head. "You know, I wonder about you sometimes."

"What's to wonder? You know, after hearing Kaff's sermon, I think I've found my calling. I can beat the lessons of the Ancients into many a penguin."

Vicar Kaff reappeared from wherever he had hidden. "Your services won't be necessary, Captain. That's not how it works. You don't beat someone into belief in the Ancients."

"I disagree, Vicar. Listening to your sermons is sometimes like being dashed against the rocks by a strong tide," Queen Gelika said, checking Thane for injuries.

"It is my faith in them which distracted the guards long enough for you to escape. Don't discount their role in our lives," Kaff huffed.

"We didn't need to fight. Another minute and they would have passed out from boredom," Gelika said with a hint of mirth.

Kaff picked up on the jest and let go of his indignant tone. "I see, My Queen. I'm happy you weren't cast to the rocks. I fear a darkness has come over the king," he said, looking at Gregor.

Gregor locked eyes with Kaff. He didn't like the direction this was going, despite rescuing the queen. "We'd better get going. Any suggestions about where?"

"I sent Lordess Tolk to the back of Kraysol. She'll be waiting for us."

Admiral Gregor averted his eyes. That was the last place he wanted to go, but it seemed his choices were slim. "Let's go then." He motioned with his flipper to Gelika.

She stepped past him, looking as if she wanted to ask him something.

"I'll tell you later," he said and followed her.

Captain Thane fell in alongside Kaff. "Let me be your apprentice or deacon or little vicar—whatever you call it. I want to stand on a mountaintop, and yell, *by the power of Huhellsus*, and have lightning fly from my beak or something."

Kaff raised an eye at her. "That's not how it works, and a vicar does not fight."

"Does a vicar make up stories about the Ancients?"

"My story, while having elements of... falsities, was based on the *true*, but little-known story of Miaska and how she came to be. It was a story my master, Vicar Orn, taught me. And as he would say, you're making my stomach hurt."

Thane opened her beak to continue, but Gregor cut her off. "Captain, when the vicar is in need of an apprentice to teach the art of lightning shooting, I'm sure he'll come for you. Until then, he did great today, and we couldn't have done this without him. So let him rest his bruised morality."

"*Humph*," Thane said, doing her best to sound affronted.

"Thank you, Admiral," Kaff said.

"No, thank you, Vicar."

CHAPTER 20

King Elinthaw stopped on a low rise overlooking the coastline. He stared across the glow of the midday sea. So eager for blood was he that he completely disregarded Hally's warning. The beach was filling with downy brown-feathered youth. Something had spooked them, but whatever it was, it had definitely not been the Royal Emperors. "Find out who called the alarm. Have them taken to the Edge." He searched the shoreline, attempting to puzzle out why the beach had been vacated. "And send out scouts. I want to know what's lurking offshore that would have frightened so many."

"Yes, Your Majesty," Grand Admiral Hally said, knowing he would be next on the Edge if he were to gloat or remind Elinthaw what he'd said before they left. "Shall we return to the execution?"

Elinthaw felt the urge to strike the penguin across the beak. "You know as well as I, they have escaped. Gather a search party. I want them found. And then I want them executed without the circumstances tradition insists upon." A faint caw from somewhere high overhead drew Elinthaw's eye. The dark, barely visible form of a Skua circled above and flew toward the mountain summit.

The king continued to stare curiously at the sky. His eyes widened. "Watch yourself, Hally," he said, stepping back. A something hit the rocks between them with a sickly *splat*.

Grand Admiral Hally looked up. "Skuas. Disgusting creatures." He walked farther down the mountain, telling Elinthaw who he saw fit to carry out the search, when he noticed the king hadn't followed. The king was examining what the Skua had dropped. "Sire, why are you so transfixed by Skua excrement?"

Elinthaw lifted his head. "Come here, Grand Admiral, and tell me what you see."

Hally reluctantly went back to examine the waste. When he realized what he was seeing, he pulled back. "This is a toe, a penguin toe. And not a chick. Judging by the size, it belonged to an adult."

King Elinthaw looked up the long trail leading to the Court of Sparroth. "Someone has recently died." He began marching up the mountain.

"But we have no way to know where the victim came from."

Elinthaw spun toward Hally. "That may be true, but if they killed one of the guards during their escape, we will have murder to add to their list of crimes. Let's go. It will be dusk by the time we arrive."

"As you wish, Your Highness." Hally chirped instructions, sending others to carry out the orders of the king. He looked at the toe once more and shivered in revulsion. "I hope it belonged to Thane."

CHAPTER 21

The group reached the Talon of Wisdom and stood in the center of an area surrounded by jutting columns of stone. Gregor turned to face the others. He looked at each penguin before him; they were all outcasts now, and he would do whatever he could to protect them "The king will stop at nothing to kill us now. Whatever happens, we stick together until we're off this island, Elinthaw is removed from power, or he dies of age. Though from what I've seen, it appears he will outlive us all. I'm sure you've all observed this; there is something unnatural in his actions. Vicar Kaff, I know you have."

Kaff shifted his eyes between the others and relinquished a heavy sigh. "There is a darkness within him, and I'm unsure as to what can be done. Vicar Orn never taught me how to deal with something like this. I can't explain, or even guess how, but his youth has returned. But this is a penguin who should have been dead ten winters ago. His age has exceeded all others."

"Are you sure about that, Vicar?" Gregor asked.

"Admiral Gregor, regardless of ability or legend, Elatha-Cadail cannot possibly still be alive. He would be nearly fifty winters old. Demon or not, to live that long is impossible. Your night terrors and sleep journeys are from the dream world."

Gelika and Thane looked at one another. "Wait, wait, wait. Demons, sleep journeys, and *Elatha-Cadail*. What haven't you told us?" Queen Gelika asked, her voice commanding but with an undercurrent of fear.

Gregor said, "I've had dreams. I… took sleep journeys, and they started after I followed Elinthaw down the path…." He trailed off. "Where did you say Lordess was waiting for us?"

Captain Thane hesitated. "The back of the mountain. Why? What's down there?"

"I don't know. Something though. Elatha-Cadail—"

"Elatha-Cadail has been dead for a generation," Queen Gelika interrupted. "I heard the stories in the king's court when I first arrived, before Elinthaw forbade us from speaking his name."

Gregor walked up to Gelika. "My Queen," he said quietly. "I was attacked by a penguin with large white eyes near the bottom of the trail when I followed the king. The following night the same penguin lured me in my sleep to the Edge. I awoke just before I stepped off. Both nights I was attacked by a Skua. If it's not Elatha-Cadail, then it's somebody remarkably similar."

"Why didn't you tell me?" Gelika asked, losing all haughtiness of royalty. "I sent you to follow him because I thought he had a mistress from the other colony or was hiding something."

"I didn't have time to tell you. And I wasn't going to ruin the moment, any more than I already had last night," he whispered. A wry look from Thane told him he wasn't being quiet enough. He straightened. "Regardless, we have to get to Tolk. Something dwells there, whether it be a penguin, a spirit, or simply a Skua, and it's dangerous."

The group followed Gregor's lead, Kaff fighting with Thane over not wanting to take up the rear.

In spite of the dire circumstances they found themselves in, Admiral Gregor was in high spirits. He felt for the first time in a long time, if not the first time in his life, he had a greater purpose. They were actually going to make a change, and if they didn't, there was nobody else he'd rather be exiled with. His spirits were dampened considerably when they rounded a sharp bend.

"Stop," the admiral said, spotting something ahead. He raised a flipper in front of Gelika, who gave him a concerned look.

Captain Thane was at his side in a second. "What do you see?" She leaned forward, trying to see what had alarmed him.

"There," he indicated with his flipper. "Come on. Vicar, stay with the queen."

From somewhere above they heard the distant caw of a Skua. Gregor shuddered. He moved closer to what he had seen, already guessing what it was. He didn't need to tell Thane what was there; she saw and ran to it. Gregor walked up behind her as she stared at was had once been Lordess Tolk.

Thane shook her head. "How? What could've done this to her."

Admiral Gregor looked at the pile of bone, blood, and torn flesh. He had only seen this kind of damage after seal attacks, and he was certain there were no predators in the mountains. The Skua's call came again, sounding closer than it had before. He had never heard of a Skua taking an adult King, but then again, he had never been attacked by one until recently.

The captain had drawn the same conclusion as Gregor, that a Skua had partially consumed her friend. "This doesn't make sense. The creature, whatever it was, even took her toes. I don't get it."

Queen Gelika arrived with Vicar Kaff nervously shuffling behind her. "Is it Lordess Tolk?"

"It was," Thane answered. "We need to find what did this to her."

"Or who," Gregor said.

Vicar Kaff protested. "Admiral, if Elatha-Cadail *is* still alive, he is beyond our power to cope with. We should leave. Now, before King Elinthaw arrives at the Talon of Wisdom."

"We can't just leave her," Captain Thane said.

"What do you suggest we do, Captain? If we try to drag her body, we'll leave a trail from here to the sea. And don't forget the king will be searching for us." Gregor looked back the way they had come. "We can't stay here tonight."

Thane looked at Tolk's body. "What's happened to the world, Vicar? Aren't there enough worries without our own kind trying to kill us?"

"Desire, whether it be for food, or authority, love or revenge, breeds chaos, Captain Thane. Chaos left unchecked festers like sand in your gut, until it destroys you from the inside. Chaos will—" Kaff stopped talking. "That's it, Admiral. Elatha-Cadail is alive, and he lives because of Elinthaw. And Elinthaw lives because of him."

Gregor stared blankly at Kaff. "The king protects him? What would he have to gain from the one who murdered his father?"

"No. They are symbiotic. Each depends on the other to survive. My Queen," Kaff said abruptly. "Has the king exhibited any odd behavior?"

"You mean beyond sentencing me to death?" Gelika quipped.

Kaff missed the joke. "Yes, My Queen. While that is unusual, is there something other than that?"

Gelika looked away. "He has always been distant, but he became especially so after my sister's capture and subsequent death. He had good days when he was energetic and days when he looked older than the sea. The latter became more pronounced after Gelida died. And yes, there is something different about him. Like something lurks behind his eyes." The call of the Skua drew her attention.

"Vicar, whatever you're thinking will have to wait. We need to leave." Thane was staring at Tolk's body. "Captain, we have to go."

Thane remained motionless until Gregor called her once more. She nodded and followed.

"Where are we going, Admiral?" Gelika asked. "We can't go back the way we came."

"We'll go to Cuasan's Beak."

"But that's a dead end. We'll be trapped," Gelika protested.

"But there's plenty of shelter along the way, too. We can stay out of sight and rest up until morning," Gregor said, trudging up the hill. "Who knows, maybe there's another path hidden along the route."

"If you mean a path straight down, then you are correct, Admiral."

"Straight is always the quickest way to go, My Queen."

"You can go first and tell me how quick… Admiral"

Gregor coughed a laugh and gave the queen a playful slap. He waited for a rebuke for the public display, but it never came. The admiral made an internal vow to give his life protecting her.

CHAPTER 22

The waning gibbous moon illuminated the path leading to the interior and the steaming caldera. A Skua beckoned from the darkness, inviting Elinthaw to join it in the gloom. Grand Admiral Hally stood nearby, awaiting orders in the search for Gelika and the others.

"It's obvious Vicar Kaff is an accomplice to the fugitives. When they are captured, they will be executed at once. No delay, no deviations. I want them dead by sunset tomorrow," the king said, eyes locked on the downward-sloping trail.

"Yes, Your Majesty," Hally answered, eager to carry out the order but feeling trepidation. "But if I may speak candidly."

The king faced Hally, causing him to take a step back. He let the silence between them hang, until the Grand Admiral parted his beak to apologize. "Of course you can."

Hally swallowed. "It's just that if we execute four of the most visible leaders at once, it could stir up doubt or even outright rebellion. And while I am all for ridding the colony of Captain Thane and the others, as much as I detest him, Vicar Kaff is our only conduit to the Ancients for the time being. He has yet to take on an apprentice."

"If you don't see my commands fit to carry out, perhaps I will add a fifth *visible leader* to the group," the king said, sounding condescending and almost petty.

Hally straightened. "Not necessary, Your Highness. My concerns were unfounded. I am gracious for your enlightenment."

"Now, if you would bring your troops to the Court of Sparroth. There are other ways off this mountain, and one of them leads through there." Elinthaw turned his back on Hally.

"As you command, Your Majesty." Hally started to leave, but waited when the king didn't follow. "Will you be there for the capture, Your Highness?"

"You should be capable of apprehending them, Grand Admiral. As you said, we are without a vicar. I will commune with the Ancients within the Talon of Wisdom." Elinthaw walked to the center of the stones. "Go, you haven't much time."

Grand Admiral Hally almost hesitated, but the king gave him a look telling him he shouldn't.

With Hally gone, King Elinthaw stood alone in the Talon of Wisdom. "Was Lordess Tolk's claw a warning or a gift?" he asked the emptiness.

A Skua swooped through the columns, landing nearby. "What is it about the K'tha that makes you pursue a fool's errand, and causes you to you abandon the execution of the queen?"

"Aren't we to attack the Royal Emperors? They betrayed us. We committed our forces, and they never returned. It was because of them that Gelida died."

"You are as pathetic as you are stupid," Elatha-Cadail said. His voice rasped like claws on stone. He turned his back and moved toward the shadows. "Perhaps there is another more worthy."

King Elinthaw fell to his stomach, gasping for breath. His eyes turned gray and blind, and his flippers curled, brittle with age. The Skua began squawking and hopping, taking flight and alighting repeatedly in a screaming dance. The king choked for words, but none came.

Elatha-Cadail called from the shadows, his voice small against the noisy bird. "But we are too deep in our plans for me to find another." He returned to the moonlight, and stood over Elinthaw. He moved in a wisp from claw to stone claw of the Talon of Wisdom until the king coughed.

Elinthaw rose behind Elatha-Cadail, wheezing and shaking. He slumped.

"The K'tha will be dealt with in time." Elatha-Cadail rushed Elinthaw, stopping before him, white eyes boring into the king's. "The claw of Tolk was neither gift nor threat. My pet was merely hungry. She does work so hard, I couldn't let such a meal go to waste."

King Elinthaw tried to turn away but was unable to move. The white eyes reflected the moonlight, appearing to glow. The pungent, coppery scent of blood floated through the air, seeming to surround Elatha-Cadail. The smell crawled up the king's nostrils, sending a wave of electric shock through his skull. The demon spun away, the Skua took flight in an eruption of screeching, and Elinthaw's eyes fluttered, fighting to stay open.

The King stood alone within the Talon of Wisdom, staring at the night sky.

CHAPTER 23

The rising sun offered no resistance to a fast approaching storm, moving in from the west. Queen Gelika stood beside Admiral Gregor, watching the blanket of smoke-gray consume the morning's blossom of color.

"We need to get off the mountain," Gregor said. "The wind will tear us off the cliff."

"Our only choice is to go back the way we came. I'm sure with Thane at our backs, it would take an entire regiment to stop us." Gelika looked at the back of the alcove where they had taken shelter the night before. "Provided she was awake for it."

Captain Thane raised her head with exaggerated effort. "You know what the Ancients said about sleeping late," she said, her voice scratchy from sleep.

"Actually I don't, Captain." Gregor said. "Why don't you enlighten us?"

Thane glanced at Vicar Kaff, who gave her a disapproving grumble in return.

"Well, Admiral, they said if a fool rises with the sun, then he will be a tired fool." She shook herself, trying to wake.

"I'm sure none of the Ancients said that," Gregor replied without looking at her.

"They said something like it, I'm sure. Isn't that right, Vicar?"

"No, Captain Thane. Nothing like that has been said by the Ancients." Kaff stepped out of the alcove into the strong wind.

"Oh yes they did, or one did. It was Claineuse, the third Ancient of Judgement." Thane stood proud of her false knowledge.

"While I'm impressed you know who the third Ancient of Judgement is, you're still wrong," Kaff said. He ignored Thane's insistence she should be an apprentice, turning his attention on Gregor. "We're going back? Then why did we even come this way?"

"I didn't hear any answers from the Ancients coming from you, Vicar. If we'd tried to fight our way back down the mountain, we'd all be dead by now." Gregor looked at Gelika. "I was too tired. I couldn't fight."

"We were all tired, and I'm wounded," Gelika said. "Thane fought hard, but even she has limits to her strength."

"Hey!" Thane said. "Mind your words, My Queen."

"As it stands, we may have caught a break. The storm should move most of Elinthaw's soldiers down or off the mountain," Gelika continued, sounding hopeful.

"I have a question for you, Vicar Kaff." Gregor said, turning the mood more serious.

Kaff lowered his head. "No need to ask anything, Admiral. I let fear take me, and I snapped my beak at you. I humbly apologize."

"Our lives have changed in a day. We have death warrants, and there's a demon penguin probably wanting to feed us to the Skuas. We're all a little stressed. Don't worry about it. But my question isn't about that. I need to know—will you fight if you have to? It might be our only way to freedom."

"My job is to educate others on the works of the Ancients, so that we may avoid evil and stand against it if we have to."

Gregor perked up. The vicar continued speaking, but he blocked him out. An idea had splashed against his head and begun to grow. The first strong gust came; it was enough to make him brace himself to keep his balance. But still he thought about the idea. "Let's move. And thank you,

Vicar."

"Thank you?" Kaff asked in surprise. "What have I done to earn your gratitude?"

"You gave me an idea. Captain Thane, I need to ask you a favor."

Captain Thane approached him warily. "The favors you ask are never good. What is it this time, Admiral?"

"Do you think you can muster the forces? And pull them away from Hally and the king's influence?"

"Hally won't be a problem, but asking some of them to be disloyal to the throne may be difficult. What do you have in mind?"

"I need you to go down the mountain alone, convince the officers to abandon Hally, and have them prepare to fight if it becomes necessary. I don't want any fatalities. They are our families and friends. Can you do this?"

"No fatalities? Not even Hally? I have promises to keep, Admiral." Thane threw her flippers up, pretending to be frustrated.

"Only if he deserves it," Gregor said, tucking his head against the wind.

"Oh, he deserves it. Just look at his face. He's practically begging for it," Thane said, moving alongside of Kaff. "Wouldn't you agree, Vicar?"

"While I must agree Hally is most surely deserving of a beating of one sort or another, I'm afraid I can't condone the killing of a fellow penguin."

"Well, Hally hasn't tried to have you killed… yet. Though I have the feeling he will soon enough."

CHAPTER 24

By the time they reached the Talon of Wisdom, snow was falling, heavy and wet, with such intensity, it dampened their voices and sight.

"Do you think you can make it?" Admiral Gregor asked Thane.

"I think I can. Once I make it around the third bend, the mountain will provide me shelter," Thane said, as serious as she had ever been.

Gregor studied her for a moment. "Don't risk your life for this. We can work out another plan. I don't want you walking off a cliff or stumbling into a sentry because you can't see."

"Admiral, my life is already at risk. If they capture us, we'll be executed. We need support, and I'll find us some. And if I stumble into a sentry, he won't like it much." She moved close to him. "So what is your plan?"

Gregor exhaled sharply. "I would say I don't want to tell you in case you're captured, but I'm sure you'd eat your beak before telling anyone." He hesitated, trying to muster his courage.

Queen Gelika stood next to Gregor while Kaff sheltered his face from the snow. "I think I already know," she said, her voice sounding strong through the wind.

Kaff pulled his head up. "What? What are we going to do?"

Admiral Gregor took a breath. "We're going after Elatha-Cadail."

Thane and Gelika nodded, and Kaff threw his flippers up in a panic.

"You can't," Vicar Kaff said. "It's suicide… madness. If it truly is Elatha-Cadail who is causing this, he is far more dangerous than anything you've faced, Admiral. He can see your thoughts, determine your dreams."

"Then we'll stay awake. This is the only way. I followed Elinthaw down there, and I was attacked by something. The king is much older than he appears, and Elatha-Cadail is even older. We need to stop whatever this is. If we don't, the entire colony is in jeopardy." Thane caught Gregor's eye. Her expression was one of masked fear. "You'll be fine. You'd better go; it'll take you a long time to get down the mountain."

"I'm not afraid for me, my friend." Thane raised her eyes at the queen. "Take care of him. Next time, you make the plan."

Queen Gelika snorted a laugh. "He's the military leader. I thought I could trust him."

"All right, all right. Go, Captain. May the spirit of the Ancients be at your side." Gregor nudged Thane with his flipper, shooing her away.

"I hope they're at my side, and they don't want me at theirs. Not yet, anyway."

After Thane had gone, Kaff turned to Gregor. "This is a bad idea. You have no idea what you're dealing with."

"I've met him in my sleep, so I do have *some* idea what we're dealing with," he said, leading the way to the trail. "What about the Ancients? Won't they protect you? Where's your faith?"

Kaff followed close behind Gregor, bumping into him. "It is their wisdom I follow, Admiral. And this…. This is foolishness."

CHAPTER 25

Captain Thane swore when she banged her shoulder into a rock. "Why do the mountains have to be made out of stone?" she grumbled, fighting her way through the whiteout.

She moved as fast as prudence allowed, sometimes stopping and feeling her way with each step. The wind pushed at her and she shoved back. Step by step she descended until she reached another bend. Her progress was so slow, she had a difficult time discerning the turns in the trail. She leaned against a large rock, hoping it would shelter her for just a moment so she could catch her breath.

Instead, the wind swirled, driving the snow, which had become sleet into her face. She tucked her head and waited it out. Several minutes later the wind relented, and Captain Thane started on her way again.

She continued to growl her complaints to the storm. "Why did they have to have a meeting place where the only access to it is a trail along a sheer cliff wall? I wonder if the king surveyed the entire island for the most inconvenient spot." She shook her head, trying to rid her mind of unproductive thoughts while trying not to let them shift to her friends on the other side of the mountain.

Before long the wind reduced in ferocity. Thane guessed she had found the third bend, and after surveying the surrounding area, she hoped she was correct. She leaned back against the cliff wall, preparing for the next section. She was past the Court of Sparroth and the king's throne, but next was a wider expanse where she would be fully exposed to the elements. She waited, reciting the Nine Ancients of Judgement for luck before she left. "Sparroth, Fain, Claineuse, Hatrenck, Carentok, Kak'tor, K' K' thon, Ortrion, and… Trivitreon. I know my Ancients. I could be vicar. What does Kaff know?"

Thane firmed her beak and shuffled around the cliff walls, buffeted by wind and snow immediately. The snow had piled so high, she had to climb up before she could head down. After she'd surmounted the first berm, she spotted movement, something dark between the curtains of snow, and she fell to avoid being spotted. "Luck of the Nine Ancients of Judgement, my tail feathers. That didn't help." She inched forward; ahead of her was a line of sentries with their heads tucked against their chests, spread across the width of the trail.

"What to do?" She searched her brain, trying to figure out another way past. Regardless of how hard she thought, no answers came forth. "I guess I'll have to go through them."

Captain Thane marched forward, sinking and nearly falling with every step. She arrived at the first sentry already tired. She practically fell into him as she tried to remain standing.

The sentry spun around, letting out a gasp when he saw her. "Captain Thane? What are you doing out here? Grand Admiral Hally said you're a fugitive. Is it true?"

It was Sergeant What's-his-beak. She couldn't remember his name, but she knew she liked him. He was a good penguin. "Only half-true. The other half is the king has gone mad. The queen, Admiral Gregor, and I are trying to stop him. We could use some help if you'd like to join us."

He stared at her through the driving snow. His beak parted, but a voice from behind stopped him.

"Sergeant Hazel, who are you speaking to?" the captain of the guard asked, peering around the sentry. "Oh."

"Fall down, Hazel," Thane said.

"I... I... don't—"

"Arrest her. Don't let her escape," the captain said, tripping through snow, trying to get to her.

Thane looked at Hazel. His eyes were wide and unsure. "I'm sorry," she said. Hazel tried to respond but never had the chance before Thane's flipper struck him with enough force to push him facedown in the snow.

The captain ordered for the guards to attack. A dozen sentries moved toward Thane, falling and standing and falling again, trying to make their way to her in the loose snow.

Thane felt herself sinking a little deeper while she stood watching. The captain was having his own problems, as he, too, had sunk nearly chest-deep in the powder. She looked at the sky, almost wishing for the sleet to return; she would have been able to stand on that. "I could wait for the thaw or for them to get to me, whichever came first, but I think I should be going."

She fell to her stomach and pulled herself with her flippers, trying to swim through the snow. At first she thought she had made a mistake, but the snow felt more compacted beneath her weight. She dug her flippers in again, adding a kick with her feet, and moved forward. She poked her head above the snow, and through a break in the storm spotted one of the sentries flailing on his back, unable to get up. She snorted a laugh, repeated her actions, and propelled herself a little farther. "And I thought this was going to be the slowest escape ever."

Her momentum carried her away. She heard the shouts of the captain telling his squad where to go. *Too late, I'm already gone,* she thought.

Thane continued her kick-and-pull method of escape, tobogganing away. She'd started on a slow incline, and she began to pick up speed. "This is kind of nice. I'll be down this mountain in no time." The incline became a steep grade, and her leisurely pace increased to a fast drop.

Rocks whipped by her at alarming speed. She dug her right flipper into the snow, creating enough drag for her to navigate a gentle curve. She heard a yelp on her left and looked in time to see another penguin fly off the trail. The others had figured it out too, or more likely copied her. It didn't matter now. All that mattered was staying ahead of the pursuit.

The sun peeked through a break in the clouds, temporarily giving her a better look ahead, but when she angled into another turn, the glare made her close her eyes. Deciding shut eyes was probably a bad idea, she opened them in time to see a protruding rock directly ahead. She dug both flippers and feet into the snow, giving her enough resistance to slow her pace. She released her right flipper and cut hard to the left, skimming the rock. A squawk from behind told her one of the pursuers hadn't been as resourceful.

Thane made a hard right, but one of her stalkers made a tighter turn and found himself alongside her. She stole a glance, and he did as well. She broke left to avoid another rock. The snow wasn't as thick here. She hoped to hear a cry of collision but was disappointed when the other penguin reappeared. Distracted, she almost didn't see a second sentry coming until it was too late. That one zipped across her path, so close he nearly grazed her beak.

A third pursuer arrived, biting at her feathers and feet, trying to slow her down and put an end to the chase. She wondered how they'd caught up when she had gotten such a great lead. A fourth flew by her, flippers neatly tucked, shifting his body weight to make subtle turns. "All right, they didn't just copy me, they improved on my idea. Two can play catch the invisible squid," she said, remembering a ridiculous Gentoo legend she had heard.

Captain Thane pinned her flippers to her side, making her body as sleek as a torpedo. She couldn't help but howl with excitement at the boost of speed. The two sentries in the lead heard her and leaned hard to the inside, hoping to hit her from both sides as she bulleted through. She quickly extended her flippers, slowing. The two in front, with no target between them, crashed into one another, tumbling to the wayside. The tail-biter sailed around her, nearly crashing into one of the tumbling penguins.

The guard to her right kept pace while the other stayed in the lead. The leader slowed, causing Thane to veer right. A call beside her informed the leader to do the same, cutting off her escape. The three banked hard into a sharp right turn, skirting the edge of a cliff, followed by an equally sharp left, avoiding a rock wall. The pursuit resumed when the path straightened, and Thane let out a heavy breath. This was getting too dangerous. It would have to end soon.

The sky darkened once more, holding the promise of more snowfall. She had to try to end the insane tobogganing. She cut right, digging her wing deep, making the turn behind the sentry to the right of her. She didn't have to look to know the others still followed.

Captain Thane found herself on a wide expanse picking up more speed. The others stayed with her and then one tried to cut her off. He hadn't adjusted to the increased speed and zipped past. He spun out of control, rolling until she lost sight of him. One left.

She tucked in tight, adding more speed, and immediately wished she hadn't. Thane flew over a mogul, feeling like the mountain had disappeared beneath her. The wide expanse turned into a near vertical drop. She hoped she could stay in control. She landed, surprised to see the other had kept pace, and even more surprised when another joined them. She knew who he was by the way he looked at her. The captain of the guard narrowed his eyes and slid in next to the other penguin.

Thane could finally see the coast in the distance. She could also see the snow line fast approaching. The others saw it too, and the sentry edged her tightly, giving her almost no room to maneuver. He stole glances at her, satisfied she would have to give up. Thane chuckled when she looked at him. "Bye," she said, and shifted her weight, hitting him with enough force to cause him to lose control.

The guard's eyes widened when he realized what was about to happen. He swiveled and twisted, and for a moment, Thane thought he might pull out of it. He didn't. He tried to brake, which started him rolling. He continued to tumble, staying with her until he went end over end down the hill, looking like an oblong starfish on its edge, caught in the surf. "Whoa. That was magnificent," Thane said, watching him careen away and out of sight.

The captain of the guard was still in pursuit, but Thane didn't care. The snow line was nearly upon her, and there was little she could do to stop. She once again dug her flippers in the snow, trying desperately to slow down. She felt the dirt beneath the thin layer of snow. Her pace began to ease, and she let out a breath, knowing she would avoid a violent ending. But the captain of the guard couldn't match her skill and crashed into her, sending them tumbling the remainder of the way, past the snowline, over the tusset grass, and into a gravelly stream.

Thane lay there, very aware of the Earth's rotation, feeling the water flow past. Eventually the ground quit spinning. She stood. The captain of the guard, only a foot away followed suit. She started laughing. An honest laugh, not a mocking laugh. "That was incredible. Look how far we came." She looked up the mountain, their starting point lost in the clouds.

The captain of the guard followed her gaze and laughed too. "Yes, that was quite a—"

"Shut up," Captain Thane said, slapping him across the face, sending him back into the stream. She surveyed her surroundings and then walked away, grumbling. "He tries to execute me, and then he wants to be my friend. Idiot."

CHAPTER 26

Kaff slid into Gelika's back, who, in turn, fell against Gregor's. "We're on a fool's quest," the vicar said after Gelika gave him a disapproving look.

The path had been dangerous before. With the snowfall hiding hazards, it had become life-threatening. Rocks slid from their precarious perches, tumbling past the group with such regularity, they learned to distinguish the noise through the tremendous gusts. In some places, the snow had completely covered the trail, forcing them to climb over the shifting piles, hoping it wouldn't pour over the edge, taking them with it.

Every once in a while, the group swore they could hear the Skua's call through the wind. None of them could figure out how a bird could fly in inclement weather. They were certain gusting wind would drive the bird into the cliff wall. But the calls came nonetheless, giving them the feeling that whatever lived here knew they were coming.

"I never said I wasn't a fool," Gregor said, trying to calm Kaff. "But we have to be getting close."

Gelika remained quiet, standing back as the males argued amongst themselves.

"Close or far matters little. We are ill prepared to face Elatha-Cadail." Kaff mumbled quiet chants, beseeching the aid of the Ancients.

"There's one of him and three of us. The odds are in our favor." He regretted bringing the queen with them. Gregor had vowed to protect her, and he was leading her into a dangerous situation. But the alternative would have been to leave her to own devices up top and the possibility of her execution. At least he could be in her presence this way.

"Elatha-Cadail lives in this region. Any advantage in numbers is trumped by his knowledge of the terrain."

"Don't be so pessimistic, Vicar," Gregor said, trying to ease Kaff's fear. "Go back to your supplications and find an answer to help us deal with this thing."

"The only answer I've received is to turn around and find another way." Once again, Kaff chanted low.

As it turned out, Gregor's assessment of distance was far from accurate. The climb down took several more hours, but as they drew closer to the bottom, the storm eased and the snowfall was replaced by mist. The change was both welcome and unwelcome. The fog hid features more than the snow. Objects appeared far away, only to be a few feet in front of them. The flapping of wings could be heard coming from somewhere unseen. The group huddled together, eyes peeled, looking for an aerial assault. When none came, they edged forward.

The ground leveled out, and Gregor stopped. "This is where I was attacked. He came from over there." He pointed toward a gap in the mist.

No threat emerged, and they moved closer to the vacancy in the fog. The daylight filtered to a haze, which was enough for him to get a better look at the surroundings. He saw a level patch of gray soil and moved to investigate. "Here. Look, there's another path. It might be another way out of this place. There's no way a penguin can climb this mountain with regularity. Demon or not, he has to have limitations."

"We've climbed Kraysol several times in the past two days," Kaff said.

The queen had had enough of the vicar's negativity. "Listen to me, preacher. The next noise that comes out of your beak better be something other than death and disaster. You're supposed to be a leader of faith, not a doomsayer. Start acting like it, or you can climb back alone."

Kaff nodded. "My apologies, My Queen. I am not above fear. I will do better for your sake."

Gregor let a whistle escape him. "Couldn't you have done that halfway down the mountain?"

Gelika shrugged. "My patience can only be pushed so far. Besides, I shared his feelings until now."

Gregor jerked in surprise. "And what changed your mind?"

"The other path. Elinthaw would go on his journeys, and sometimes he would return with gray mud stuck on his claws. The mud is gray that way. If this Elatha-Cadail really is here, we have to put an end to him. Not tomorrow or a moon from now. We have to do it today."

Emboldened by the queen's words, Admiral Gregor stood tall and stared at the gap in the fog. "Then let's do it."

The trio walked into the void, which turned out to be a passage to the edge of the caldera. Gravel sporadically trickled down the path from the slope on their left, and to their right a pool of water sat in the crater. Their feet crunched on the fresh gravel, surprisingly brittle beneath their weight.

"We're not sneaking up on anyone with this noise," Gregor said. "But I have a feeling he knows we're here anyway."

"I don't like your feeling, Admiral," Kaff whispered behind him.

"I don't want to talk about my feelings anymore," Gregor said, transfixed on a cave ahead of them. "It looks like we're here."

Gelika and Gregor exchanged looks and slowly moved toward the opening.

"How do we know this is the place?" Kaff asked, looking behind him in case something followed.

Gregor examined the entrance, paying attention to the ground. "Look, there're fresh droppings on the rocks, and there are pinfeathers. We're where we are supposed to be." He looked down the dark tunnel, spotting the faintest glow deep within. "There's light coming from somewhere inside."

Kaff stopped at the entrance, and Gelika didn't move with much enthusiasm either.

Admiral Gregor faced the two. "You don't have to go in with me. You can wait here. This was my idea; I can see it through alone."

"No you can't," Gelika said. "We started this together, we'll finish it together. Right?"

Both of them looked at Vicar Kaff. "I'd rather not meet my end the same as Lordess Tolk. I'll go with you. The Ancients will be with us."

"I hope they are," Gregor said, and they entered the gloom.

CHAPTER 27

The air became more stagnant and heavier with moisture the deeper they went. Trickles of condensation flowed down fissures in the rock. The comparative warmth felt thick in their lungs. A sulfuric smell hung in the air, which Vicar Kaff described as the stench of abandoned eggs, arguing that the Skua's brought them, taken from unwary parents. The others ignored the unfounded tales and pressed forward.

Admiral Gregor's senses heightened. Gelika remained stoic for reasons only she knew. The Vicar's recitations of protection from the Ancients became louder. "Your noise will send us all to the Ancients if you don't quiet down."

The tunnel curved and twisted, as if bored by a monstrous worm, and pale light glimmered off the moisture, which flowed down the walls. They rounded a gentle curve, arriving at a junction where the tunnel split in three directions.

Admiral Gregor let out a long breath. "Any suggestions?"

"Your guess is as good as mine," Gelika said, finally breaking her silence. She spun around, looking back the way they had come. "Did you hear that?"

Gregor looked at Kaff, who shook his head. "Hear what?"

A quiet hiss crawled up the corridor.

"That," she said. "What is that?"

The hiss transformed into a whispering groan.

Kaff began his recitations in earnest, quickly delivering every blessing that crossed his panicked mind.

"Shut up," Gregor said. "I can't hear where it's coming from."

The whisper turned into a scratching voice. "Which way to go?" a voice said behind them.

The trio turned in unison, with Kaff burrowing his way between Gregor and Gelika.

"Make your choice." The voice said came from the tunnel to the left. The group turned in that direction.

Gregor started walking toward the sound, but Gelika stopped him, shaking her head.

"The queen doesn't want you to go that way, Admiral," the voice said from the right-hand tunnel. "Does she care for you? Or did the king's affection for her sister push her to you? It must have been hard knowing the king wished you were someone else. And now he wants to kill you. An unwanted queen is such a pathetic thing to see."

Queen Gelika locked eyes with Gregor. They turned toward the center tunnel.

"She wants you to come this way," the voice said a little louder. "Please do. I would like that very much."

They stopped once again. "Any ideas, Vicar?"

Kaff was too busy with beseeching the Ancients to answer.

"Vicar Kaff. Do you know what your mentor, Vicar Orn said just before I took his life?"

"You didn't kill him. He died a natural death," Kaff said shakily before returning to his petitions.

A laugh swirled through the tunnels. "He begged me to take you instead. You always disappointed him."

"A demon doesn't know truth. He knows only lies," Kaff said, standing tall, calling to Huhellsus for aid.

"The Ancients don't dare enter my mountain," the voice said from above. "The Ancients fear me!"

The group turned to see the white eyes of Elatha-Cadail behind them. Kaff cried out, and the form of Elatha-Cadail disappeared, replaced by the Skua. The bird struck Kaff, and Gregor and Gelika ducked out of the way.

The landed, hopping on the ground, looking between Gregor and Gelika. It flew at the queen.

Admiral Gregor pushed her aside, taking a bite on his neck for the favor. He snapped his beak at the bird, catching it by the tail. He fought against the bird's powerful wings and fell back, using his weight to fling the Skua against the cave wall.

Gelika stumbled away, hitting something other than stone. She lifted her head, staring directly in the eyes of Elatha-Cadail.

"I have a king, and now I have a queen to match."

Gelika slumped, fighting to stay on her feet. He abandoned his fight with Skua. "Kaff, do something!" He hurried toward her, but the Skua pounced on his back, pecking him with ferocity.

Vicar Kaff started to run, but stopped. "I'll live to regret this," he said and rushed Elatha-Cadail, breaking the queen free.

Elatha-Cadail moved in a wave of darkness before Kaff hit him. "You're wrong, Vicar. You won't live at all." He struck Kaff, sending him tumbling against the wall.

Gelika stumbled toward the Skua on Gregor's back. With her strength failing, she fell on both of them. The Skua squawked and hopped away, taking flight down the left tunnel.

Gregor thanked her but saw the confusion in her eyes. "We have to get you out of here." They got to their feet and began to run.

"Kaff," Gelika said. Elatha-Cadail was standing over him.

Admiral Gregor didn't know what to do. He had been wrong; he didn't have the strength to defeat such a creature. It was like it knew what he was thinking; it could see what he would do. He remembered what Kaff had told him: that Elatha-Cadail might have been born as an Oracle. "Kaff, close your mind to him. Don't think. That's his power over you."

Kaff shook his head, trying to block out the specter.

Elatha-Cadail started to laugh. "How fortunate am I to kill two vicars in my time."

Vicar Kaff began reciting the old legends, focusing on them instead of what surrounded him.

The white eyes turned toward Gregor and Gelika. "Let's see if you can practice what you preach, Admiral." Elatha-Cadail sprang at the two.

They closed their eyes, bracing for an impact that never came. When they opened them, Elatha-Cadail was gone.

Gregor looked around, unsure what had happened. "Come on, Kaff, on your feet. We have to go."

No sooner had Kaff stood when the mountain rumbled. "Now," he yelled to the vicar. He pushed the two in front of him, urging them to go.

They ran, but Gregor stopped, unable to take another step. A beak drew itself across his neck. Paralyzed by the bright eyes of Elatha-Cadail inches from his own, he could only stand and watch.

"The queen is mine now. She will do my bidding. She will betray you as she betrayed Elinthaw. She will betray you all."

The mountain vibrated, and Gregor fell free. He looked at the others, who were watching him. "Go!" he yelled and rushed to join them in their escape.

They moved as quickly as they could, and burst from the mouth of the cave. Admiral Gregor made sure the others got to their feet. "We'll take the other way," he said, guiding them to the muddy path.

Steam erupted from the cave behind them, and the group fled to safety.

CHAPTER 28

The trio made their way through a rocky ravine, fighting the terrain and weather, eventually emerging near the base of Mount Kraysol. The wind tore across the sloping hill, carrying the last remnants of snow. The gray sky thinned, giving hints of the coming night. They made it no farther than the edge of the beach when they noticed something was amiss. They ducked into the low vegetation, spying on what was taking place.

"What are they doing?" Vicar Kaff asked, panting heavily, the day's events having taken their toll on his strength.

In the distance, penguins stood in lines several rows deep. King Elinthaw loomed at the head of the formation with Grand Admiral Hally at his side. Behind them were over a thousand soldiers, standing at attention, ready to do the king's bidding. Youthful brown penguins huddled together on the far side, watching the spectacle.

"The king is up to something," Gregor answered.

"A good or bad something?" Kaff asked.

"It doesn't look good. The soldiers are tense," Gelika said. "Do you think they captured Captain Thane?"

Gregor shook his head. "I doubt it, but whatever happened, it looks like the king is going to make an example of someone."

Two soldiers came forward and took a penguin from the lineup. After a heated exchange, the soldiers pushed the penguin to the ground before the king. Hally stepped forward, appearing to say something to the penguins in the lineup. He looked at Elinthaw, bent down, and stabbed the prone penguin in the back with his beak. The line of penguins began to move toward the king, but the superior group of soldiers moved forward, giving them pause.

"The king has lost his mind. We have to stop him," the admiral said. He started to stand, but a rustling in the tusset grass to his left made him think twice. He looked closer and saw Captain Thane's head poke out between two clumps of the thick tusset. Gregor's shoulders slumped in relief. He scooted across patches of snow and dirt and rolled into the patch next to Thane.

"You almost blew our cover," Thane reprimanded her commanding officer.

"I'm glad you made it too," Gregor quipped. "What's going on here?"

"One of the officers I contacted to help us proved disloyal to the cause. The king sent his suckling to round up the rest of us. About a hundred managed to escape to the sea. We made our way back to land, and we're waiting to make our move. That's when you showed up." Thane looked away. "That was Sergeant Hazel they executed. We had a run-in, but he defected to our side. Apparently the king has lost his forgiving nature."

"The king is dead," Gregor said.

"You got that right. Hally will be too."

"What I mean is Elatha-Cadail has his mind. I don't know how; it's beyond my comprehension. Something to do with the abilities of an Oracle, but he has him."

"So why not kill this Elatha-whatever?"

"We tried, but he wasn't there, so to speak." Gregor turned his attention back to the display below.

Thane shrugged. "We should move before he makes an example of someone else."

"Where are the others?"

"Here and there," she said, indicating the hillside with her beak.

On closer inspection, Gregor noticed that all the snow wasn't snow but rather penguins on their backs, presenting their white bellies as camouflage, blending nicely with the fresh snowfall. "You're brilliant, Captain Thane."

"Yeah, well, I know," she said sheepishly.

Gregor laughed. "Always humble. You seem to have things well under control. We're vastly outnumbered, you know."

"Some of his loyalists aren't so loyal. We'll be all right."

Gregor nodded in approval "When you give the order to attack, the queen and I will move on Elinthaw."

"You're making me commander?" Thane asked, tilting her head.

"Yes, Commander Thane. Now get to work before we're seen." The call of a Skua came from above, and Gregor growled, looking at the sky. "Though I think we've already been spotted."

CHAPTER 29

Grand Admiral Hally spun toward the sound of Thane's troops moving down the hillside. The lines of traitors perked up and began to move toward him. He nudged King Elinthaw. "This way. Fall back into the ranks."

"A king doesn't run from a fight," Elinthaw snarled.

"But a king lets pawns weaken the opponent before he strikes. Move." He pushed Elinthaw into the mass of loyalists moving forward.

They ducked and shoved their way through until they reached the rear lines. The soldiers watched the fracas. "What are you doing? Get in there—attack. Protect the king from these insurgents."

The lead penguin looked at the two of them. "Remember Thane's orders. Kill Hally and capture the king," he shouted above the cacophony, and the turncoats advanced.

"Uh-oh," Hally said. "Back! Back into the center."

Elinthaw looked at Hally with eyes burning with rage. "They won't kill me. I shan't return the favor."

The lead penguin approached, and Elinthaw moved to meet him. He speared him through the throat and knocked him aside. "Fight or die, Grand Admiral."

Hally watched the crowd of penguins approach, remembering their orders to kill him. "I'll get reinforcements," he said, ducking into the mass of supporters.

King Elinthaw ignored Hally's cowardice. He turned on his enemies, looking on them with the eyes of Elatha-Cadail. The Skua flew overhead, screaming at the carnage, eager for a meal. Three penguins on the hillside made their way in his direction. Another soldier came at him, and he dispatched him much the same way as the previous challenger. "Gregor," he hissed and moved to meet them.

Hally shoved his way through the crowd, striking at the rebels with beak and flipper. He slapped them down, finishing them off with his beak when he could and leaving them underfoot when he couldn't. "Kill me? I'm the Grand Admiral, and when Elinthaw meets his end, I'll make myself king."

A rebel penguin came at him, nearly knocking him to the ground. They spun to face each other, and the rebel came at him again. Hally met him with a flurry of slaps, which the other returned. They separated, readying for the next round. "You fight well. It's a shame I have to kill you now." The rebel lunged at him with his beak. Hally ducked under the attack, coming up under him and driving his beak the rebel's throat. He pulled back, wiped the blood on his victim's chest, and pushed him over, satisfied with the kill.

He continued to attack, becoming increasingly confident with each victory. He fought his way to the edge of the fray, and his confidence wavered. Captain Thane was there, fighting her way across the field of battle, inching in his direction. Under cover of the brawl, Hally waited to ambush her.

CHAPTER 30

Thane moved closer to the center of the fight. She spotted Hally but lost sight of him when another penguin came at her. She head-butted the penguin back but didn't strike him. "Stand down! We shouldn't be fighting each other. I don't want to hurt you. I will, but I don't want to."

The other penguin hesitated. He lifted his flippers as if ready to slap, then lowered them. "The king will put me to the Edge if I refuse to fight."

"The king will fall and then what will you have?"

While the penguin stood in contemplation, another came at her. She met him with a spinning slap that stunned him and followed up with another from the other side. She bull-rushed him, using the back of her head to hammer him across the beak, knocking him out in an instant. She looked at the thoughtful penguin. "This could be you. Is this what you want?" She waved her flipper at the unconscious penguin.

"I'm going to go for a swim and rethink my life."

"That's a good idea," Thane said, watching to make sure he did so. She looked at the melee, trying to spot Hally. "Now where did you go, you little guano speck?"

She pushed past a pair of hard-slapping combatants and separated another, shaking her head when one appeared ready to lance the other with his beak, which made them reconsider. A pair of loyalists came at her, but knowing her reputation, a warning glare was all it took to make them back down. Thane paused before entering the mass, seeking out her quarry. His head popped out from behind another penguin and quickly ducked back in. She snorted in disgust and a bit of amusement, she went toward him.

Hally appeared and came at her, yelling with beak agape, ready to bite. Thane stepped aside, slapping him on the back of his head.

Hally skidded to a halt and turned. "I've been looking forward to this for a long time," she said. "Well, not really a long time, but for a few days now. I never liked you, but I've only recently come to hate you enough to kill you."

"Enough talking. You sound like one of those accursed Gentoo," Hally barked. "Prepare to meet your match, Captain."

"Bah! I don't sound like a Gentoo. Do your worst, or your best, but I think they're both the same thing in this case."

Hally attacked with a barrage of slaps, which Thane easily avoided. He cursed, coming at her again, this time with more control. He slapped her across the beak with a lucky strike. His eyes glinted with satisfaction until Thane's left flipper met his face with a hit that required no luck at all. Thane stared at him, waiting for more.

The Grand Admiral rushed her, slamming into her, driving her back. Thane grunted and shoved back, nearly toppling Hally. Undeterred, he tried once again, mixing slaps with attempts to stab her with his beak.

She parried his efforts and slapped him back. They stood in a clearing on the edge of the skirmish. She let out a long sigh. "This is boring. I don't like boring." She spun, her flippers windmilling at her side, striking Hally three times before he could react. She assaulted him again with a combination of slaps, forcing him back, trying to get clear. Thane's attacks were relentless; over and over she pummeled the hapless Grand Admiral, adding pokes of her beak to her arsenal.

With no other recourse, Hally tried to run away. He scrambled up a rocky hill, tripping over loose stones and slick earth.

Thane stayed with him, biting and tormenting him as he tried to flee. Growing tired of the chase, she bit him on the back of his neck, tearing a small amount of flesh away.

Hally squealed in pain, twisted back, and managed to hit Thane.

Thane took a step backward to adjust her footing, but the wet soil gave way, causing her to tumble down the small slope. She landed against rock, hitting hard enough to daze her momentarily.

Hally took a step to run away. He looked at her, lying on her back, defenseless and on the edge of consciousness. He moved toward her.

He bounded down the slow grade, and stood over her, gloating. "It appears luck is on my side today, Captain. And unlike you, I've been looking forward to this since I first met you."

He reared back and brought his head down, intending to drive his beak through her neck. Thane rolled at him, causing him to stumble forward, landing beak first against the rock. He screamed in pain when his beak cracked on the stone.

Thane stood. "Mm. That has to hurt," she said, looking at the tip of his beak hanging sideways just below the nostril.

Hally rested against the rock, trying to scoot himself up on his feet, his head hanging over the back the rock. He muttered something Thane couldn't understand.

"I have no idea what you said." She stepped beside him, appraising the mess he had become. "Do you remember what I said the other day about snapping your neck and shoving it up your squidhole, and all of that nonsense?"

Hally nodded.

"I'm many things, Hally, but I'm not a liar. Bye."

Hally could only turn his head slightly before Thane fell on it with her full weight, feeling the gristly snap of his neck beneath her. She stood, studying her work. She nudged the body off the rock, examining it for a while. "Ah, I guess I am a liar. I just don't see any way to shove his head up his squidhole."

CHAPTER 31

King Elinthaw approached Admiral Gregor and Queen Gelika on the edge of the battlefield. Gregor, showing no signs of being intimidated, marched straight toward the king.

"It was disappointing I couldn't kill you on the mountain. Your strength of will is impressive. However, you will still die."

Admiral Gregor stared at him. "Are you Elatha-Cadail?"

The king let out a sickly laugh. "I am who you see before you. My mind was weak with age and loss. My true queen had died, and I went to Elatha-Cadail to have him bring her back for me. I pledged my throne to him if she would only live. But I had no throne to give. Escalefact had already pledged his first surviving son to him, and by association the throne, if the demon would not return in his lifetime and let him have a fledgling to survive."

Gregor stepped closer. He knew the king was trying to stall him with the story. He had to act soon. Gelika started walking to the other side of Elinthaw while Kaff stayed in the bushes.

"King Escalefact wasn't lured over the Edge. He chose his fate. He couldn't live with the guilt of giving his son to the monster. Escalefact betrayed the entire colony for generations because of his own weakness." Elinthaw moved toward to Gregor. "The throne survives on betrayals, Admiral. Isn't that right, My Queen?"

Gelika stopped, glaring at the king. "It was your betrayal of the colony to the Royal Emperors which cost your *true* queen her life."

Elinthaw laughed. "Even if you have survived this, Admiral, Gelika will betray you too. She is the emissary to the Overlord. She petitioned our inclusion in the alliance. And she seeks to rejoin that alliance. In time, you would have seen."

"Behind you, Admiral! Behind you," Vicar Kaff shouted from the hillside.

Gregor turned and was met by the Skua. The force of the impact sent the admiral to the ground. The bird landed on his chest and tried to peck his eyes out. Gregor rolled, and the Skua flew up, ready for another attack.

Gelika used the commotion to go after Elinthaw. She hurried toward him. The king faced her, his eyes turning white.

"Such a waste," he said. "Spending your life in the shadow of your younger sister. The sister you saved after your parents abandoned another hatchling. I can't imagine the hardship of watching your betrothed fawn over the flesh of your younger sister. But no matter. Now you have my full attention. In fact, I might just get rid of the old penguin in favor of you."

Gelika struggled to move, Elatha-Cadail's hypnotic eyes immobilizing her. "I never cared about your affection. I was forced to be queen because no one else would have you. I've hated you since I've known what it was to hate," she choked out the words, almost struggling for breath.

"Hate is such a petty emotion. It emboldens the weak. It makes them feel like they have power over that which they cannot control. I've never known hate, but I have made a partner of its sister... revenge. And at last, Escalefact will pay in full for his actions."

Gregor ducked under the next swooping attack. The bird soared back, taking another swipe at him. Gregor lashed out, trying to catch it as he had earlier. He failed, and the Skua cawed, mocking his failure. Gelika was in trouble, but he knew the bird would make another run at him. "Where is Kaff?" he grumbled. "I could really use some help about now." The bird came at him low and fast. There was little he could do but brace for the impact.

As it closed the distance between them, Vicar Kaff stood from his hiding place in a patch of tusset grass. "I'm here, Admiral," he yelled. The bird had no time to alter its course and crashed into Kaff's back, sending them both tumbling to the ground.

"Great! Fall on that bird. Don't let it get away," Gregor called.

Confused, Vicar Kaff twisted his head back and forth. He let out a noise of resignation and pounced. The Skua squawked and screamed beneath him, but Kaff stayed on top.

The king searched for the Skua, alarm in his eyes, and saw Gregor coming after him.

Gregor ran into Elinthaw, sending him to the ground.

Gelika fell away, released of the hypnosis the white eyes had held over her. She casually strode to where Elinthaw and Gregor fought one another, trying to get to their feet before the other would have the advantage.

Elinthaw won the race, knocking Gregor to his back. "Ah, Admiral, your capacity to resist can only take you so far. Now it's time to die."

Gregor nodded. "I agree, Your Highness. It is about time you died."

Elinthaw scrunched his white eyes in confusion and then they went wide when Gelika stabbed her beak into the back of his neck. He gasped when she struck again. The king fell when she struck a third time.

Gregor joined Gelika, and they watched the white eyes fade to gray as the king's body withered to a husk of its former self.

"What just happened?" Gregor finally asked.

"We killed the king," Gelika said, finding a patch of snow to clean her beak.

Kaff joined Gregor. "I believe Elatha-Cadail never fully had dominion over Elinthaw. Perhaps his will was too strong, or maybe the demon lacked something. Either way, he's gone now."

Gregor looked at Kaff. "Where's the Skua? Did you kill it?"

"It got away," Kaff said quietly.

The admiral growled. "How could you. You had it."

"It bit me," Kaff said.

"So? It bit me a lot. I can't believe you let it escape."

"But it bit me. It hurt." Vicar Kaff continued to plead his case.

Gregor walked off, joined by Gelika, who shook her head at Kaff. Thane came toward them with the sunset at her back. "Right on time," Gregor said.

"As always," Thane replied. "What'd I miss?"

Gregor moved off, and Thane fell in alongside him, with Gelika on his other side. Vicar Kaff struggled to keep up. Gregor let out a tired breath. "Well, we did kill the king, and we fought some kind of evil oracle demon thing—oh! And Kaff got bit by a bird."

"It really hurt," Kaff protested.

The four walked across the beach, past the opposing factions, who were discussing reconciliation.

"I could use a swim," Admiral Gregor said. The group fell into the surf.

CHAPTER 32

Gregor, Gelika, Thane, and Kaff sat next to Stone, watching the final hints of daylight disappear into the sea.

"You can take your Bakorpheous stone back." Gregor tossed the piece of glass at Kaff's feet. "I don't think I'll be using it again anytime soon."

"I'm glad it was of some use to you, Admiral," Kaff said, nudging Stone's curious nose out his face.

"It really sort of was, Vicar. The thought of it did pull me from that sleep journey."

"The Ancients were with us," Kaff said, closing his eyes.

"You know, Vicar, I still think you could use an apprentice. I *do* know a lot about the Ancients," Commander Thane chimed in after popping her eyes open from a brief nap. "Besides, you could use some protection."

"While I have no doubt of your knowledge, Commander, to become a vicar, one must never have broken someone's neck and stuffed their head up their squidhole."

"I never stuffed Hally's head anywhere. It wouldn't work. It was a physical impossibility."

Gelika scooted next to Gregor, ignoring Thane and Kaff's argument. "I was thinking. We can become life-mates after I step down from the throne."

Gregor looked at her from the corner of his eye. "We could have Kaff do the ceremony right now and not wait."

Gelika sniffed a laugh. "I really wish we could, but I'm required to appear in mourning after the king's death. It wouldn't be right."

"I know, I know. But I think it's time to be rid of some of these ridiculous traditions, starting with the Order of Kings."

"I'll leave that to my successor, but we can restructure it elsewhere. We don't know if Elatha-Cadail lived or not. We never actually saw him in his physical form. I think it's nearing the time for our colony to leave."

"True, but where would we go?"

Gelika cleared her throat. "That decision I'm leaving to you."

Gregor didn't respond.

"You're the only one I trust to lead a survey team and find us a new home. You can continue the search for Kiley while you're looking."

"I forgot about that problem. His treason still needs to be answered for. I'll think about it. What do you think, Stone? Should I go to sea for a winter's time?" Stone snorted a flatulent reply. "I don't think he's keen on the idea."

"He can go with you," the queen said, eliciting several honks and grumbles from the old bull.

"We'll leave it for tomorrow. How's that?"

"That, Admiral, sounds fair." Gelika sighed, turning her gaze to the sea.

Gregor followed her lead, his eyes getting heavy. Thane and Kaff had already fallen asleep. He was drifting off when he heard a sound. It was quiet beneath the roar of the sea, but he heard it nevertheless.

Gelika picked up on his tension and became alert. "What do you see?"

"I didn't see anything. I heard something."

Thane was on her feet in an instant, ready for action, and Kaff scooted closer to Stone.

The three stood silent and ready, eyes wide, waiting for something to approach out of the night. After several moments, they eased. "I thought I heard the Skua," Gregor said. "I'm sorry. Go back to sleep."

"There are a lot of those things on the islands. It would be hard to know which is which," Gelika said.

"Yeah, I guess we'll have to live with that." He was thinking about sitting when he heard the sound of wings against the wind. A Skua swooped in, squawking and trying to bite Gregor.

Thane came forward, trying to find an opening to bite back, but the flurry of wings prevented her from getting close. Gelika tried as well with the same outcome.

The Skua beat its wings harder, staying at head level, biting at Gregor repeatedly.

The sound of a crunch was be heard above all else. The Skua screamed as a second crunch came. And then it went silent. The crunching continued as Stone chomped and finished his meal.

Kaff emerged from hiding, and the others stared at the Elephant Seal. Stone swallowed and rested his head on the sand.

"Thank you," Gregor said.

Stone grumbled for several seconds.

"Did you know they ate birds?" Thane asked.

"I thought they ate fish and squid," Gregor said. "I guess he expanded his pallet. He's coming with me on my survey."

"No, he can stay here," Thane said.

"Perhaps I'll take your nest when you leave, Admiral," Kaff said. "Stone will need the company."

Thane protested, arguing with Kaff long into the night.

Gregor and Gelika leaned into one another and slept.

CHAPTER 33

Lord Keese stepped into the center of the Talon of Wisdom. The clouds blew across the moon, dampening the light, throwing shadows across the stones.

White eyes appeared between the columns, and Elatha-Cadail emerged. He approached Keese, standing before him as silently as the stones. "Lord Keese," he rasped. "I'm glad you could come."

Keese wavered on his feet, nodding.

"I am in need of someone who desires power and eternal life. Would you be the someone I'm looking for?" His beak grazed Keese's throat, gentle and dangerous.

"I desire all of that and more. What do I need to do?"

"You just need to look at my eyes." Elatha-Cadail's eyes widened.

Keese trembled and fell back unconscious. After a moment, his eyes fluttered open, bright and full of life.

More from Rockhopper Books

Rise of the Penguins Saga

Rise of the Penguins - Book 1

Whispers of Shadows - Book 2

The Warlord, The Warrior,
The War - Book 3

The Royal Creed - Book 4

.